SECRET OF THE FOREST

by

H. J. GOODYER

THE CHILDREN'S PRESS
LONDON AND GLASGOW

This Impression 1966

CONTENTS

CHAPTER ONE

THE GREEN WOODPECKER

"NOT FAR NOW," said Uncle Arnold. "Only another four or five kilometres."

He increased speed a little, but not for long. Even the Daimler's feather-pillow springs couldn't dampen the incessant "dub-a-dub, dub-a-dub" from the cobbles on that second-class German road.

"Shouldn't be surprised if we didn't see the house after the next couple of bends," Uncle Arnold continued. "It's pretty high up, and you can see a goodish bit of the road from it." After a moment he went on ruminatively, "Of course, that's why the old Bosche had been using it as a strong-point, and it was pretty badly knocked about by mortar fire and so on before our chaps took it over. The first time I saw the place it was a dickens of a shambles."

Roger half turned in the front seat and drooped an eyelid at me. We'd already heard the story twice and it looked as if Uncle Arnold was going to start all over again. But neither of us said anything. The old boy did so enjoy telling it.

"Anyway, shambles or no, the Colonel decided to use it as his Regimental Headquarters for the night. It was pouring with rain and parts of the roof were still intact. It was an awful mess inside of course, broken glass and chunks of ceiling all over the floor, and it was when we started to clean up the stuff that I came across the photograph. It was of two men in hunting kit, leaning on their rifles and looking jolly pleased with themselves, and in a big flourishing hand it was autographed —in German, of course—"Affectionately, Hermann Goering." One of the chaps in the picture was old Hermann himself, no doubt of that."

We had topped a rise as he was speaking, and were now running down towards a straggling village. It had a forlorn and uncared for appearance, but I think this was due chiefly to the fact that there had been a lot of rain, even for early March, and the farm-carts had brought in so much mud from the fields and daubed it over the cobbles. We saw few tractors —I don't think the farmers were very prosperous.

"Kallendorf," Uncle Arnold was saying, before Roger or I could read the name from the yellow signboard. "My word, I remember Kallendorf." We swished through the village; chickens flapping and dogs barking in all directions.

"About three kilos to go," said Uncle Arnold. "What was I saying?"

"You found the photo," prompted Roger.

"That's right. Well. The next morning my batman produced a hat he'd found mixed up with a lot of junk in one of the bedroom cupboards. It was one of those Tyrolean affairs with a feather, and inside were stamped the initials, H.G."

Uncle Arnold stretched himself in his seat, chuckling happily to himself. "H.G.," he repeated. "Well, wouldn't you have put two and two together and got the same answer as I did?" He turned to include me as well as Roger in the question.

"Sounds fair enough," I said.

Uncle Arnold nodded and turned back just in time to avoid a large brown cow that was standing in the middle of the road and mooing at us resentfully.

"Yes. Particularly after a couple of our signallers roped in an old family retainer who'd been hiding in the forest and who confirmed that the gallant Reichsmarshal had used the house as a shooting lodge only three or four weeks earlier. Three or four weeks earlier, you know," said Uncle Arnold, tapping Roger on the knee. "You'd hardly credit it, would you. Germany on her last legs and the fat loafer goes on a shooting trip. It's no wonder they lost the war.

"We had an American liaison officer attached to us at the time, Texan he was, called Johnny Vermont. My, how he coveted that hat—you know how Yanks are about souvenirs. For the rest of the day my man Potter was never where I wanted him—Johnny was all the time getting him into a corner somewhere and trying to bargain with him. In the end he had his way. I never asked how—it seemed better if I didn't know—and Johnny came proudly down to dinner wearing Hermann Goering's hat."

We were climbing again now, the ground rising gradually at first and then more steeply from the cobbled track. The green pasture land was giving way more and more to scattered pine woods that merged into dense forest on the really high ground. You could see the road winding up for several miles until it was lost in the misty darkness of the trees ahead.

Uncle Arnold bent over the wheel, squinting up at the ground on our left.

"There you are," he said suddenly. "Just below that big horse-shoe-shaped wood. Wonderful position. Sheltered by trees all the way round."

"It looks a big place," said Roger, peering out through the side window. "Surely it hasn't really got a thatched roof?"

Uncle Arnold chuckled in a pleased way. "It has. Or it had, anyway. Though last time I saw it, sixteen years ago, it wanted more than a little doing to it. You see, what happened was this. We moved in on 3rd May. We spent the next day doing nothing very much and fully expected to be moving on the day after. But the day after," said Uncle Arnold dramatically, tapping Roger's knee again, "was 5th May."

"The day the war ended," said Roger brightly.

"That's right, my boy. The signal came through ordering all hostilities to cease at 08.00 hours, and of course there was a certain amount of jubilation. Johnny Vermont's reaction was to lay on a hot bath for himself—said he wanted to start the peace clean. Potter boiled him up three kettles of hot water and at half past seven that morning I could hear Johnny splashing away and singing at the top of his voice. Then the fun started.

"It seems a group of German paratroops—real die-hard Nazis—decided to make a party of it and blaze off all their ammo. before eight o'clock. My word, they went to town on us. By some miracle no one was killed, though it's hard to imagine why. Then they got a direct hit on the roof with an eighty-eight millimetre and what was left of the bathroom ceiling fell in on Johnny." Uncle Arnold chuckled fruitily. "You've never seen such a sight. Johnny coming out of that bathroom without a stitch on, covered with soap and plaster, and that ridiculous hat stuck on his head. I'll never forget it as long as I live and I don't believe he will, either. I reminded him of it when I ran into him in Liverpool last year and he told me it was six weeks before he felt really clean. Poor old Johnny, how he must have suffered. He loved his soap and water."

I said, "He booked our accommodation here, didn't he?"

"That's right. His father—Pop, he calls him—is by way of being a big man in the oil business and Johnny runs the office in Hamburg. He does a lot of running about, and one day he was driving this way and found our old R.H.Q. was being used as a sort cf private hotel. So when we fixed up this week's holiday I wrote and . . ."

Rounding a sharp bend we had overshot a small turning to the left and Uncle Arnold pulled up with a squeal of brakes.

"I'm pretty sure that's our turning," he said, and reversed until we could read the faded signpost. Or rather, until I could.

"Hochwald, two kilometres," I said.

"Yes, yes," said Uncle Arnold. "But what about the little sign—the new one underneath? I never could make out this ridiculous Gothic lettering."

"*Der grun Specht*," I read in my best accent. "And below that it says 'Gasthof.' That means guest-house," I explained.

"That's it all right," said Uncle Arnold. "Johnny said they'd re-named it—something about a woodpecker. The Speckled Woodpecker, that'll be it, eh, Jimmy?"

"Not quite, Uncle," I said. "The *Specht* is the woodpecker bit. The Green Woodpecker, it means, really." But I don't think he heard.

If the road we'd just left was bad, this was worse; winding, rutted and barely wide enough for the big Daimler. I wondered what would happen if we met another vehicle coming down. But we saw none, saw in fact no sign of life at all as we continued to climb, drawing closer to the horse-shoe-shaped wood, whose western tip now reached down on our left hand. This would be the Hochwald, I thought; the "High Forest."

"The really amusing part," said Uncle Arnold, who had never really lost the thread of his story, "was the sequel. You see, with the ending of hostilities, Johnny was recalled to his regiment and it wasn't until a day or two later, when I was going through some intelligence reports, that I came across one that our own Intelligence Officer had done on this retainer chap who was still hanging around the premises and making himself generally useful. I'd only known him as Gruber until then, but when I saw his Christian name was Hans, it suddenly struck me." He smiled round at us, waiting to see who was going to be the bright boy.

"Hans Gruber—H.G. The initials on the hat," suggested Roger diffidently. He did it rather well, as if he'd never heard the story before but had arrived at the answer by following it with such close interest.

"Right first time," said Uncle Arnold. "See it, Jimmy?"

"Oh yes," I said. "But Johnny Vermont went on believing it had been Goering's?"

"I doubt if I would have had the heart to tell him anyway. As it was, I didn't see him again until last year. Apparently he's got it mounted on a solid silver stand in his office, with a neat little card that says, 'This hat was worn by Reichsmarshal Hermann Goering on numerous shooting expeditions, the last being only three weeks before his capture by U.S. forces in May, 1945.' " Uncle Arnold chuckled. "Poor old Johnny. If he did but know, I expect old Hans merely used it now and again when he was doing the garden."

"He wouldn't mind much about losing it then," said Roger.

"Good lord, no. Hans didn't have anything to complain about. You see, with the war ending, we settled down to a more regular way of life and took Hans on as a mess waiter. Kept him for about a year too, until the regiment was disbanded. No, with all the unemployment there was in Germany, Hans was sitting pretty. I wonder what happened to the old thing—I always had a soft spot for him."

We swung round a sharp right-hand bend and suddenly

there was the house, squat, sprawling; its grey stone and thatched roof giving it a centuries-old appearance. It was built on a curving spur of rocky ground about two hundred yards back from the road and the low hedge that encompassed the garden made no pretence at hiding the gentle terraces, the rockeries, the rose beds and the well-kept lawns.

We passed through the wrought-iron gates and drove slowly up the long drive, the gravel crunching pleasantly under our wheels. Uncle Arnold kept up a constant monologue as if we were a conducted tour. "That's where we had the cookhouse . . . the Regimental Aid Post was just about there . . . 'course, the lawns didn't look like this then. . . ."

We had barely stopped outside the main door, studded with nails like a medieval castle, when a boy of about Roger's age— eighteen—came running out to take our bags. He wasn't liveried, but he wore one of those peaked German army-type caps and it gave him a look of being in uniform. Perhaps this impression was emphasised by the fact that he didn't smile, even when Uncle Arnold tipped him, only muttering, "Danke, mein Herr," as if he grudged the word of thanks.

Our greeting at the reception desk was quite different. There was a man sitting there writing in a large book who jumped up briskly as we appeared and leaned forward on the desk, a look of intensely respectful questioning on his rather florid face. He was a big man, well over six feet, with closely-cropped greying hair and very blue eyes.

"Er—good afternoon," said Uncle Arnold, speaking rather loudly, and with a faint un-English accent which I suppose he thought helped when speaking to foreigners. "My name is Keene, Major Keene. You speak English?"

"But assuredly, Herr Major. Delighted to have you with us. Holtz." I heard his heels click together as he bowed stiffly from the waist.

"I beg your pardon?"

"Good afternoon, Herr Holtz," I said, to help the thing along.

"Oh, I see," said Uncle Arnold. "Your name, eh? Well, Holtz, these are my two nephews, Mr. Roger Keene and Mr.

James Keene. I believe a Mr. Vermont booked accommodation for us for the week.

Holtz reached for the large book and turned it for Uncle Arnold on the desk, handing him a pen at the same time.

"That is so, mein Herr. Two rooms, on Mr. Vermont's instructions. Willi!"

The young chap who had brought in our bags reappeared from somewhere close at hand and Holtz handed him two keys from the rack at his elbow. "Numbers 6 and 7," he said to Uncle Arnold. "Both in what we call the east wing. On a fine day it is possible to see the Harz Mountains from these windows. Not to-day, though," he added with a wry glance outside. It had begun to drizzle again.

"See the Harz, can you?" said Uncle Arnold. "Must be quite a step. Thirty-five, forty miles?"

"*Sechzig*—sixty kilometres."

"Mm," said Uncle Arnold. "Nice district. Matter of fact," he went on, in a burst of confidence, "I've stayed here before. My regiment was deployed in the fields down there and we sited R.H.Q. in this very house. In point of fact we were here when you . . . that is, when the war finished."

I'd been watching Holtz, but his expression never changed, not by the merest flicker.

"Indeed, mein Herr. You will find a few changes, then."

"By Jove, I do. I must say you've got it done up very comfortably. This hall, for instance, dark oak panelling and polished wood floor and so on. Almost like an English pub."

And with this tremendous compliment Uncle Arnold nodded briefly and picked up his raincoat from the counter.

"I trust you will be very comfortable, mein Herr, and enjoy your stay with us," said Holtz. "Either my wife or I will come shortly to make sure you have everything you require."

Uncle Arnold nodded again and stalked off after Willi, with Roger and me trailing behind.

CHAPTER TWO

CURIOUS BEHAVIOUR OF A WAITER

OUR ROOMS were very nice, not elaborately furnished, but with big, comfy beds and log-fires burning in the grates. Roger and I were half-way through our unpacking when Uncle Arnold came in to see how we were getting on.

"I think we shall be all right here," he said. "Clean, that's the main thing. And warm." He went over to the fire and stood with his back to it and his legs astride.

"Holtz seems a decent enough chap, but I don't care for that lad of his. Surly lout. He'll be lucky to get any more tips out of me."

"Is he Holtz's son?" I said.

"I rather think so. I asked him where the bathroom was and he just looked blank and went off saying something about 'mein mutter.' That's mother, isn't it?"

"Yes."

"Yes, well I hope she's a bit more helpful. You expect hotel staff to be able to speak bit of English. Actually, the bathroom's just opposite you. There was an old boy coming out as I came in here. Felt I knew his face, but somehow I couldn't place him. Kind of military look he had, sort of Prussian old school. You know, you felt he ought to be wearing a monacle."

There was a knock on the door and Uncle Arnold called "Enter." A woman came in, small, plain and a bit faded, but with a pleasant smile.

"Major Keene?" She dropped a little curtsy.

Uncle Arnold inclined his head. "That is correct."

"My husband ask that I should visit with you to inquire if you are satisfied, mein Herr." Her accent was much stronger than Holtz's and her English more laboured.

"Quite satisfied, Frau Holtz. If the cooking's up to

the standard of everything else we shall be very comfortable."

"Thank you, mein Herr. We shall try to see that the Herr Major is not disappointed. If there will be anything further . . . ?"

"We should like some tea, if that's possible."

"But assuredly. In the lounge, if you please. At once I tell the waiter."

She dropped her little curtsy and turned to go, but as she reached the door Uncle Arnold said, "Oh, just one moment, Frau Holtz. I wonder if you can tell me who the man is I saw in the corridor just now. Not very tall, slight build, clipped moustache, walks with a limp."

For a moment she looked nervous, frightened almost, glancing over her shoulder as she said, lowering her voice, "But that must be the General von Tarkenheim." She swallowed and then went on a little tremulously, "You—you know the Herr General, perhaps?"

"Eh? No, no. Just wondered, that's all. Thank you, Frau Holtz. We'll be along for tea directly."

She hesitated, then turned and went out without another word, closing the door very softly behind her.

"I thought I knew his face," said Uncle Arnold. "Newspaper pictures, about six or seven months ago. He'd been given a command in the new German Army and then suddenly resigned on the eve of a big NATO conference. There were hints that he was involved in some shady racket or other but they never pinned anything on him—not enough to bring him to trial, anyway. Oh well, there's not much harm he can do here."

I said, "And yet Frau Holtz seemed almost—well, scared, when you asked about him."

"You may know German, Jimmy, but you don't know the Germans. They all have this awe of the officer class. Born in them, you know; there's nothing anyone can do about it. Well, come on, who's for a cup of char?"

The lounge was a pleasant room leading off the entrance hall and had been furnished for comfort. There was a deep pile carpet and eight or nine big easy-chairs which made the room look smaller than it really was. The dark oak occasional tables had a gloss on them you could see your face in.

We settled ourselves by a pair of big french windows overlooking the garden. We might have been the only occupants of the hotel, everything was so quiet. But somehow there was nothing restful about the silence; it was more like the brooding hush that precedes a storm.

After a few moments the door opened and a waiter came in carrying a tray. He was elderly, small and stooping, and his face had a wizened look. I found myself thinking of the little stone gnomes you see in people's gardens.

Uncle Arnold was sitting facing the window, so that he didn't see the waiter until after he'd set down the tray. Then he sat up with an expression of pleased surprise and exclaimed, "Well, if it isn't old Hans Gruber. Well, bless my soul! How are you, Hans, you old rascal?"

Hans started back from the table and I heard him catch his breath with a little frightened whimper. I looked at him in astonishment. His face had gone a sort of dirty grey colour and he was trembling a little.

Uncle Arnold was obviously delighted to see him and didn't appear to have noticed anything unusual. "Well, well, well," he said heartily. "I never expected to find you here, Hans, though we were talking about you only a little while ago. Couldn't keep away from the old place, eh?"

But Hans was incapable of answering. For a moment or two his mouth worked as if he were trying to speak, then without a word he turned away and rushed towards the door.

Uncle Arnold was flabbergasted, but he quickly recovered. He swung round in his chair and bawled out, "Hans!"

The little waiter had reached the door and at first I thought he would ignore the summons, but he hesitated, stopped, and then came slowly back, his eyes on Uncle Arnold, imploringly, like a whipped dog's.

"What on earth's the matter with you, man?" demanded Uncle Arnold. "You remember me, don't you? Major Keene?"

I stared at the bent old figure standing there, the ill-fitting clothes, the tremulous mouth, the imploring eyes, and I thought I'd never seen anything more pathetic. At last Hans spoke.

"Herr Major . . ." His voice was low and husky. "Forgive, please. But, Herr Major . . ." He glanced over his shoulder and then went on more quickly, "A favour, I beg. Forget that you have known me. Please, Herr Major, Holtz must not find out."

Then stepping back a pace he went on loudly, "A thousand pardons, mein Herr. I bring you the China tea at once," and scuttled off.

Uncle Arnold turned back and stared from one to the other of us. "Well, if that doesn't beat the band," he said. "Has the old fool gone dotty? I don't like China tea, anyway."

I said, "I suppose it was all he could think of on the spur of the moment to explain your calling him back."

"That's as may be, but what the devil's he got to be ashamed of? Or more to the point, what does he imagine I know of his murky past that his employer mustn't know?"

"He doesn't look the type to *have* a murky past," said Roger.

"Well, of course not. Anyway, the security boys gave him a pretty thorough screening before they'd let us employ him. Apart from that he was a jolly good mess waiter, and in my experience absolutely honest. That's why I can't understand what's got into him. Matter of fact," said Uncle Arnold reminiscently, "he used to rather dote on me. I remember once . . ."

Just then the door opened and Hans came in again, carrying a teapot on a tray. He looked more composed but was obviously determined not to be drawn into making explanations. As he set the pot down Uncle Arnold began, "Now look here, Hans, I think I'm entitled to know . . ." but Hans only murmured, "Excuse please, Herr Major," and withdrew, closing the door behind him. Only he dropped a folded paper into Uncle Arnold's lap as he passed his chair.

Muttering "Confounded impertinence," Uncle Arnold smoothed out the half sheet of paper and read it aloud. "I come to explain to-night. Please not to speak of this to Holtz." The childish, painstaking handwriting was as pathetic as the writer.

"I can't make head or tail of it," said Uncle Arnold irritably. "I think the fellow's gone stark, raving mad."

At that moment there came the sound of light footsteps on the path outside the french windows and a girl came by, walking towards the front of the house. She was wearing a light raincoat with a bright silk scarf at her throat, and she seemed to be about my own age, which at that time was sixteen.

She glanced into the room and momentarily her eyes met ours. Then suddenly she stopped, her hand went up to her mouth to stifle a soundless gasp, and she was running back the way she had come.

Uncle Arnold thumped his fist on the table, making the teacups rattle.

"Well, if that doesn't beat all," he exploded. "There's Frau Holtz with the jitters about von Tarkenheim, Hans scared out of his wits about Holtz, and now here's some strange girl takes one look at us and runs for her life. What *is* going on?"

I got up and stood by the window. It was raining hard and darker than it had been all day. There was nobody to be seen, but in the failing light the dark mass of the Hochwald seemed to be closing in on us.

I shivered slightly and went back to finish my tea.

CHAPTER THREE

THE SMILING DUTCHMAN

"PERSONALLY, I think Uncle's right," said Roger. "Frau Holtz has got some weird sort of thing about Generals, and as for old Hans, well he's just plain barmy, you can see that."

Somehow I didn't think it was quite as simple as that, but long experience has taught me that arguing with Roger is like banging your head on a brick wall, so I merely said, "And the girl?"

"Don't ask me. Girls of that age are always a bit hysterical," said Roger loftily. "I wouldn't pay any attention to that at all."

It was about half past six and the rain had stopped, although the sky was still grey and overcast. Roger and I had come out for a stroll round the garden while Uncle Arnold was writing letters in his room.

We came up from the ornamental garden that stretched down to the road and began to walk along the flagged path from which the girl had looked in on us. From here you could see right down into the valley and the outlying farms of muddy little Kallendorf. We walked on, and turning the angle of the wall at the rear of the house, found ourselves standing in an open courtyard.

Originally, it was clear, that the house had been roughly square in shape, but more recently an extension had been built on to each wing so that the building now formed a U, with the arms reaching out towards the Hochwald.

From the attempt at conformity—grey stone and small windows—I guessed that the east wing extension was composed of bedrooms lying along the corridor beyond our own rooms. The work on the west wing, in plain brick, with large modern windows, had been done to accommodate a spacious dining-room and kitchen; from where we stood we could see Frau Holtz, with another man and woman, bustling about

21

with pots and pans. A delicious smell of roasting chicken floated out through the open windows.

My mouth began to water. "What time's dinner?" I said.

"Any time after seven. Are those the garages?" And Roger began to walk towards two low wooden out-buildings which lay thirty or forty yards from the house, in line with the kitchens.

"Holtz told Uncle he'd put the car away. I just wanted to make sure she's all right," he said, by way of explanation.

I smiled to myself. It was far more likely that Roger wanted to see what other cars were stored there. He has a passion for them, especially the foreign makes.

We strolled over to the nearest building and tried the door. It was ajar, but it was a moment or two before we realised it was the sliding sort. We got our hands round the edge and pulled, and it slid back easily on well-oiled runners.

It was poorly lit inside, with a single electric bulb over a bench in the far corner. There was only one vehicle in there—a very dirty, mud-spattered truck rather like a jeep, and working at the bench, apparently tightening something with a spanner, was Willi Holtz.

I was about to say to Roger, "Better try next door," when Willi looked up and saw us standing there. He dropped his tools and came running to the door, shouting, "*Gehen Sie weg! Es ist verboten!*"

As he came up to us I saw that his face was drained of colour. He went on repeating, "*Verboten, verboten,*" as he grabbed the door and dragged it shut. Roger and I stood gaping at each other and listening to the sounds of bolts being drawn. Then silence.

"Well, what on earth was all that about?" said Roger at last. "What was he jabbering about?"

"Telling us to go away. Said it was forbidden."

"He really is the end, that lad. I'm going to speak to his father about him. Absolutely no manners at all."

I said, "He looked quite pale with rage. Or fright."

"For goodness' sake don't start all that again. They can't all be scared stiff. Come on, let's look next door."

We found the Daimler safely tucked away in the farther out-building and Roger quickly assured himself that all was well. But what really interested him was her stable companion, a big, low-slung Mercedes. It was five to seven before I could get him away, and then only by pleading starvation.

I glanced at the first garage as we passed it. The door was still closed and there was no sound of movement.

I said, "I wonder what he was doing in there that he was so jolly anxious we shouldn't know about?"

"Funny you should say that. I was just thinking the same thing." Roger looked doubtfully at me for a moment, then he said, "You didn't happen to see what he was working on, I suppose?"

I shook my head.

"Well, I got a glimpse. No more than that, but I could have sworn it was a diver's helmet. Now what the dickens would he want with a diver's helmet in the middle of Germany?"

"You can search me," I said.

"You can search me too. But if you want to know what I think," said Roger seriously, "I think they're all raving mad, the whole lot of 'em."

Uncle Arnold had finished his letters and was sitting in an arm-chair by the fire with a glass of sherry. He said he was far too comfortable to move for ten minutes at least, so we settled ourselves down and told him of the odd behaviour of Willi Holtz.

"Up to no good, I'll be bound," was his comment, when we'd finished.

"More than likely, Uncle," said Roger. "But why a diving helmet? Are there any big rivers nearby?"

"None that I can remember. No, you must have been mistaken, Roger. You say there was a little Volkswagen in there too. I expect he was fooling about with some part of it and didn't want his father to know."

"I suppose it could have been the air filter," said Roger doubtfully.

"Something like that. Well, I'm certainly not going to lose

any sleep worrying what pranks Willi Holtz is getting up to. He'd better not start taking *my* car to pieces, that's all."

Uncle Arnold drained his glass and with a heavy sigh heaved himself out of his chair. As he put the glass down he said, "When I sent for this I rather expected Hans to bring it. I thought he might be able to get some of these explanations off his chest. But Frau Holtz brought it herself, so we're no wiser."

" 'I come to explain to-night,' is what he said," I reminded him.

"Exactly. Well, I hope he isn't planning to come and knock me up after I've gone to bed, that's all. He won't get a very sympathetic reception if he does."

As we walked towards the dining-room I was thinking that although none of us admitted to taking any of these little mysteries seriously, it was curious how we all kept harping on about them.

The dining-room was quite large, as I've said, containing eight or nine tables, with space for several more, but that evening only four tables were set, all at the kitchen end of the room, I suppose to make it easier for serving.

No one else had arrived for dinner, but Hans was in position and he directed us to the corner table. He was calm, but plainly embarrassed, so to make it easier for him I started a conversation with Roger. Or, to be more accurate, I mentioned the name of a new type of air liner which had had a lot of attention in the papers and left the rest to Roger.

As Hans handed him the menu, Uncle Arnold looked at him steadily for a few seconds. Hans lowered his eyes and began to fidget with his feet. Uncle Arnold opened his mouth to speak, changed his mind and turned his attention to the menu.

We were half-way through our soup when the General came in, accompanied by the girl who had looked in at us as we sat at tea. They came straight to the table in front of ours, the General marching as if on parade. At his table he greeted us with a stiff half-bow before turning to pull a chair out for the girl, who had kept her eyes averted and now sat down with her back to us. Hans was ready to assist the General into his own chair.

I wondered idly why two more tables should have been laid. Possibly one was intended for Holtz and his wife, who might be expected to dine later, but that still left one unaccounted for, and we had seen no other guests. But it didn't seem important and I concentrated on enjoying the food, which was very good indeed.

It was about eight o'clock and we were just finishing our sweet, a simply gorgeous concoction with a sort of coffee-walnutty flavour and lashings of whipped cream, when I was given the answer to my unspoken question.

The man who came in was unremarkable except for his teeth, which gleamed whitely like a toothpaste advertisement. He was of medium height, medium build and wore unassuming clothes of reasonably good cut. He was about thirty-five or perhaps a little more and he looked as if he might be a Civil Servant, or something of that sort.

He paused when he reached the General's table and flashed his teeth in what I felt was a slightly mocking smile. "*Guten Abend, mein General,*" he said, and then, with a somewhat exaggerated bow to the girl, "*Guten Abend, Fraulein.*"

Neither of them returned the greeting, neither looked up. The smile disappeared and the newcomer leaned over the General's table and whispered something in his ear.

The General was very angry, I could see. His face had gone a dark red and his fingers were drumming on the table. He said something in a low voice to the girl and they both rose. After a moment the stranger drew back to let the girl pass, and she took the General's arm. Then with tremendous dignity they walked out of the dining-room.

I happened to glance round at Hans just then and I got a bit of a shock. He was as white as a sheet and his face wore much the same expression as it had when Uncle Arnold first greeted him.

But I wasn't given time to speculate on this because the stranger turned from the General's table and came up to ours, treating us also to one of his flashing smiles. (I soon found that he rarely closed his lips completely—presumably he couldn't bear to hide the teeth.)

"I believe I have the honour of addressing Major Keene," he said, with a formal bow.

Uncle Arnold didn't look very pleased. "My name, sir," he said briefly, "but I'm afraid you have the advantage of me."

"Konrad, Major. Paul Konrad. We have, I think, a mutual acquaintance. Mr. Vermont, of Euro-Tex Oil."

Uncle Arnold brightened considerably. "You know Johnny Vermont?"

Konard bowed again and did some more teeth flashing. "Very well," he said. "I saw him only last week, and when I mentioned that I should be staying here for a few days he begged me to make myself known to you and give you his best wishes."

Uncle Arnold was already on his feet and holding out his hand. "Only too glad to meet a friend of Johnny Vermont's," he said heartily, and then, after he'd introduced Roger and me, "Won't you join us? I'm afraid we've just about finished eating, but . . ."

Konrad sat down with alacrity in the vacant chair. "With very great pleasure, Major. I lunched late, so if I may, I'll just join you in a cup of coffee."

Uncle Arnold nodded and signalled to Hans. I watched him as he came slowly to the table. Konrad seemed to fascinate him—he couldn't take his eyes off his face. And there was something in those eyes, deep down, that I wished I could have read. Anger, was it? . . . fear? . . . hate? Or a mixture of all three? With an effort he addressed himself to Uncle Arnold. "Herr Major?"

"We'll have coffee now, Hans. And bring an extra cup, please."

"At once, Herr Major." But as he went off I had the impression that his mind was on more important matters than serving coffee.

"Are you in the oil business, too, then, Mr. Konrad?" asked Uncle Arnold.

Konrad laughed gaily. "No such luck. No, I have merely

a civilian job with a department—a rather dull department—of NATO. I have an office in Hanover."

"Oh. Sort of interpreter?"

"As you say, Major. A sort of interpreter."

"I see," said Uncle Arnold. "Are you German, may I ask?"

Konrad hesitated only fractionally before he replied, "No, Major, I am Dutch." Then with another smile he went on, "Tell me, are you staying long? There is much sight-seeing to be done in these parts."

Uncle Arnold explained that we had only a week, but that we planned to spend a day in Hanover, another in Brunswick and also to do some walking in the Harz Mountains. Konrad nodded approvingly.

"Excellent, excellent. The mountains are beautiful at this time of the year. But I wonder . . . this part of the country is famed for its boar hunting. Might we perhaps arrange some sport before you leave?"

"A boar hunt, eh?" Uncle Arnold glanced at Roger and me and we nodded encouragingly. "Sounds a rattling good idea. Do they still hunt regularly, do you suppose?"

"They are sure to. I have never actually stayed here before but I will speak to Holtz about it. He will know."

"Yes, of course. Are you on holiday yourself then, Mr. Konrad?" said Uncle Arnold.

Again that fractional pause, then, "I suppose you would say that I am combining business with pleasure, Major." Konrad flashed his teeth and got up. "Thank you for the coffee. We shall speak of this again when I have talked to Holtz. If a hunt is not already planned it is possible that he may arrange something."

"Good," said Uncle Arnold. "Splendid."

Konrad still lingered. "I suppose strictly speaking I should speak to our host first, but as you may have seen, the General is a little touchy this evening."

I suppose we all looked a bit puzzled.

"Our host?" said Uncle Arnold.

"But yes. Didn't you know. General von Tarkenheim has owned this house for years. He still does."

CHAPTER FOUR

WILLI ASKS FOR TROUBLE

WE WERE ALL a bit tired and turned in early I read a couple of chapters of a book, but by ten o'clock I was feeling thoroughly sleepy and I was just getting down between the sheets when there was a knock on the door and Uncle Arnold came in.

"Oh, sorry, Jimmy," he said. "Hope I didn't wake you."

I said no, I hadn't been to sleep.

"The fact is, I've got old Hans with me in there. I thought you chaps might like to hear this yarn he's pitching me—blessed if I can make head or tail of it. Don't bother if you're tired, Jimmy. Perhaps Roger . . ."

Roger put down the engineering manual he was reading. "Of course, Uncle," he said.

I said, "Don't go without me. I hate missing anything."

Hans was standing in the middle of the room, shifting from one leg to the other, and generally looking as jittery as a cat with kittens.

"Well now, Hans," said Uncle Arnold. "I should like my nephews to hear this explanation of yours. Quite frankly, it sounds a bit thin to me."

Hans said earnestly, "Herr Major, I never lie to you. You must remember. Never, never have I lied to you."

"No, that's true enough," said Uncle Arnold, sitting down on the bed. "Sit down, you two. Now then, Hans, let's have it again, just as you told me before. Don't be nervous, man. We shan't eat you."

Hans swallowed a couple of times and then began in a rush. "It is as I say, Herr Major. For thirty-five years I am the Herr General's servant. Before the war we are living in Berlin and the Herr General is coming here for the sport maybe once every month and me with him. Very happy in those days, Herr Major."

"I don't doubt it," said Uncle Arnold dryly. "Go on."

"Then comes the war, and Berlin is being bombed, and so the Herr General sends me here to keep order. Sometimes he is able to spend a few days resting and sometimes he is lending the house to another officer who wishes to shoot the boar."

"Nice war some people had," commented Uncle Arnold. "Well, get on, Hans. We arrived and found you lurking in the forest. Start from there."

"I am hiding because I am afraid of the shooting," said Hans simply. "Then you are kind to me and give me a good job, and after you got home I have another job in British headquarters in Hamburg. For all this time the Herr General is retiring, but in 1954 he is given new post and I go to him to say may I serve him again." There was real emotion in Hans's voice as he went on, "The Herr General is very pleased I come back to him and I serve him and the Fraulein Grizelda until last year when there is the trouble. . . ."

"Fraulein Grizelda—that's the girl we've seen," explained Uncle Arnold. "His niece, didn't you say, Hans?"

"Yes, Herr Major. Her father, he is killed in the fighting in Berlin." Hans paused, then took a deep breath and went on almost fiercely, "Last year there is much wickedness and the Herr General is blamed. . . . Herr Major, I swear to you that he is not guilty of these crimes. There are those who . . ."

"Look, Hans," said Uncle Arnold gently, "I don't really think we can go into all that now. All we want to know is why Holtz mustn't know I've see you here before."

"A thousand pardons, Herr Major. Of course. When the Herr General is dismissed his post he tells me he cannot keep me longer and I am to look for another job. I go as waiter in a big restaurant in Berlin but I am not so happy. Then in December comes a letter from the Herr General saying that this house is now a hotel and telling me to apply to come as waiter. I am to see Herr Holtz who is appointed manager, but I am not to say I am the General's man. This is very important."

Hans paused and Uncle Arnold said, "But why not?"

Hans was silent.

"Oh, come on, man. Surely he must have given you some explanation. Didn't you ask him?"

Hans hesitated and then said awkwardly, "One does not demand explanations of the Herr General. One obeys orders, that is all. But Herr Major, if Holtz finds out that I was here in 1945 he will know I am serving the Herr General and . . ."

"And the Herr General will be angry," said Uncle Arnold irritably. "All right, Hans, if that's all you want to tell us. . . . I shan't say anything, so you can relax. But I don't mind telling you I think the whole thing's distinctly odd."

There was another pause and Hans looked horribly uncomfortable. But I think he was about to speak again when there was a knock on the door.

"Come in," called Uncle Arnold. The door opened and Paul Konrad's flashing teeth appeared, followed by the rest of him.

"I beg your pardon," he said with a slightly puzzled air. "Perhaps I intrude?" I suppose it looked as if Hans was on the carpet for some misdeed.

"Certainly not," said Uncle Arnold. "That's it then, Hans. Breakfast eight o'clock sharp for all of us." Hans bowed and slipped away.

"I mustn't stay," said Konrad, as I got up to give him my chair. "I came only to say that Holtz will try to arrange the boar hunt for Thursday—the day after to-morrow. I hope you will be able to join us."

"We should like to very much. Though we've no guns, of course."

"I believe that can be arranged. Holtz is to let me know to-morrow. You will be going out, Major?"

"Yes, we thought of running down to Goslar. I should like the boys to see it."

"Goslar. Ah yes, a delightful town. So much of the medieval so well preserved. . . But forgive me. You must be tired. We shall perhaps meet again at dinner?"

"By all means," said Uncle Arnold.

"And I shall no doubt have more news for you. Good night, then, gentlemen."

And Konrad effaced himself, but even after he'd gone his smile, like the Cheshire Cat's grin, seemed still to be in the room with us.

"Should be rather fun," said Uncle Arnold. "I've never hunted wild boar, but I believe it's a very exciting sport. Well, I suppose we ought to get some shut-eye."

As we got up to go he said, "By the way, what did you think of this so-called explanation of Hans's."

"I think he's more or less telling the truth, you know," said Roger. "After all, you said yourself the average German has this awe of the officer class. His not to reason why, and so on."

"What do you say, Jimmy?"

"I think he's keeping something back," I said, with some hesitation.

Uncle Arnold smiled. "I expect you're both right," he said. "A bit of both, eh? Good night."

We were all going along to breakfast together when Uncle Arnold said, "Hang it, I meant to get the map and check up on the route over the breakfast table. Do you mind, Jimmy. It's in the right-hand pocket of the car."

I went out by the small door which led on to the courtyard at the end of our corridor and walked over to the garages. There had been a wonderful change in the weather during the night: the sun was already clearing a slight mist and you could feel the promise of spring in the air.

The first garage, where Willi did his tinkering, was shut up and silent. I went on and pushed open the sliding door of our own garage. Both cars were still there, Uncle Arnold's Daimler and the Mercedes, but I could tell the Mercedes had been moved since I was last there. I wondered idly whom it belonged to—Holtz, the General, perhaps even Konrad.

I opened the door of the Daimler and felt in the pocket. No map. Expecting to find it in the other door pocket I got into the car and reached across from the driving seat. Still no map. The only other possible place was the pigeon-hole in the dashboard. I was sorting through this when I became aware that Willi Holtz was standing in the garage entrance and gazing intently towards the forest. I wasn't feeling particularly interested in Willi just then, and I was just getting out of the car, having satisfied myself the map certainly wasn't there, when he spoke.

"Where have you been?" he demanded in German.

I realised he wasn't addressing me, for he didn't even know I was there, but although I'm not as a rule given to eaves-dropping I stayed where I was to see who the harsh and aggressive words were meant for.

A moment later the General's niece, Grizelda, appeared in the doorway.

Willi repeated his question, thrusting his red, loutish face close to hers.

Drawing back a pace but holding her head high, she said quietly, "Please let me pass."

He laughed unpleasantly and grabbed her wrist. "Answer my question first. Where have you been?"

"I have been walking, that's all. Let me go, please."

"Walking in the forest, eh? Why? Why walking in the forest?" He twisted her arm savagely and she gave a little scream.

I couldn't stand any more. I scrambled out of the car and ran to the door way. Willi turned in amazement as I came up. I grabbed him by the shoulder and spun him round. "Leave her alone," I said.

He spluttered for a moment and then came out with a filthy stream of German. I hit him in the mouth as hard as I could and he went down with a crash against the garage door.

Grizelda gave a little gasp and then she was running towards the house. For a few seconds Willi stayed where he was, but he was more surprised than hurt, and when he got to his feet and came back at me I thought I was in for a rough time. He was three inches taller than me and a good two stone heavier.

But I overestimated Willi's prowess, or else under-estimated my own. He rushed at me with his arms flailing like wind-mills. I side-stepped and caught him a beauty on the left ear. He stopped short, puffing and blowing, and I got under his guard, if he could be said to have a guard, with a left to the body. For a moment he glared at me, then he suddenly lashed out with his boot. But I was ready for him. I grabbed his foot and yanked it upwards. He went down with a crash that might have been heard all over Lower Saxony and this time he stayed down.

As I walked back to the house I reflected that rescuing damsels in distress was all very well, but it was nice to have them on hand to murmur words of gratitude when you'd succeeded in slaying the dragon.

CHAPTER FIVE

THE HOLE IN THE WALL

BUT I WAS doing Grizelda an injustice. When I came into the house again by the little door I found her waiting for me in the corridor.

"Thank you very much indeed," she said in perfect English, looking at me shyly. "I do hope you're not hurt."

I grinned at her. "Not a bit," I said. "Just lucky I happened to be there. Not a very nice character, friend Willi."

She said, "He's hateful—hateful."

"He certainly is," I said. "I hope you'll ask your uncle to speak to his father about him. What on earth makes him think he can go around behaving like that? Like a——" I was going to say "Nazi," but I thought it might not be tactful. "Like a gangster?" I finished.

She hesitated, and a cloud passed over her face. Then, "Perhaps—yes, perhaps I will," she said.

"I should jolly well think . . ." I was beginning hotly, when there was the sound of footsteps and Roger appeared.

"Oh, hallo," he said. "I was just coming to give you a shout. Uncle's remembered he brought the map in with him after all and put it in his room. I'll get it."

"Hang on," I said. "Fraulein, this is my brother Roger. I'm Jimmy, by the way. Jimmy Keene."

Roger raised his eyebrows a shade but he said, "How do you do, Fraulein," very gravely, and took the hand she extended.

Grizelda obviously thought some explanation was due. "Your brother and I had a somewhat—unusual introduction," she said. "He saved me from some very unwelcome attentions."

Roger looked at me, his eyebrows going up again. "Willi Holtz," I said briefly.

"Oh, indeed? And you—dealt with him?"

"He wasn't making much of an effort to get up when I came away," I said with a rather self-satisfied smirk.

Roger clapped me on the shoulder. "Well done, old son. Well done."

Grizelda said quietly, "I must go now. Thank you again, very much." She smiled at me, briefly and shyly, then turned and walked away down the corridor.

Roger grinned at me. "You seem to have made quite a hit, old man," he said. "But I'm jolly glad you sorted Master Willi out. He certainly asks for it. What was he up to this time?"

"I'll tell you later," I said. "No need to bother Uncle Arnold with all this. Hadn't we better go and get his map?"

We spent an extremely pleasant day in Goslar, with its fascinating splendour of ancient buildings, and Uncle Arnold was an enthusiastic guide, though I couldn't help feeling he was more interested in where the Officers' Club and the N.A.A.F.I. were in 1945 than in what might have been there in 1495. After lunch I had the opportunity of a quiet talk with Roger and explained my set-to with Willi Holtz.

"But it's fantastic," burst out Roger when I'd finished. "Do you mean to tell me the girl's just going to keep quiet and say nothing at all to her uncle about this horrible youth and his horrible way of going on? Just let him get away with it?"

"He didn't get away with it altogether," I reminded him.

"No, but you never know when the next time's going to be. I mean, look at the way he went on at us. That alone would have got him the sack anywhere else. Seems to me he's got her so scared stiff she's just afraid to report him."

"Somehow I don't think so," I said. "Anyway, she said she might."

"Why only 'might'?"

I said, "I don't know, but I think there's more to it than just being scared of Willi Holtz. I've got an idea there's something going on."

"What sort of something?"

"I don't know," I said again. "Something odd, that's all."

"Lord, here we go again. You always were a chap for making mysteries. All right, what's the theory?"

I said, "I haven't got a theory. These peculiar things we've noticed—they don't even begin to hang together. But we *have* all noticed them. It's no good trying to put them down to my imagination."

"Well? Go on."

"You mean you want me to go over them all?"

"You know you're dying to."

"All right, to begin with there was Hans. Either he's lying, and there's something he's afraid of Holtz finding out about, or he's telling the truth, and the General's got somethi⁀ ⁀ hide."

Roger said, "It sounds a bit far-fetched. You don't expect a hotel proprietor to have guilty secrets from his manager."

"You don't expect him to go around snubbing his guests either. But that's what the General did to Konrad last evening. Anyway, let me finish. Take Willi. He practically throws a fit because we venture into the wrong garage, and then goes for his employer's niece because she's been for a walk in the forest. Frau Holtz gets the jitters when the General's name is mentioned and, funniest of all, Grizelda runs for her life when she sees us sitting in the lounge. Six things altogether, and they're all jolly queer."

Roger thought for a moment and then he started ticking them off on his fingers.

"Point one. Hans got the job here by false pretences; made out he'd been at some swishy hotel for donkey's years and knows he'll get the sack if Holtz finds out he was lying. Point two. The General's touchy—Konrad said so himself; not used to running a hotel and fed up with strangers wandering about in what used to be his own home. Also explains why Frau Holtz is afraid of him, if he loses his temper from time to time. That's point three. Point four—Willi. Quite simple—he was fooling about with his father's car. Point five—oh, something similar, I expect; for all I know he's been pinching things from the house and got them stacked away in a hollow tree.

There you are," said Roger carelessly. "All quite easily explained, really."

"I wonder," I said. "Anyway, there were six points. What about the last one?"

"The girl? I said at the time it didn't amount to anything. She may have suddenly remembered something she'd forgotten. Her handbag, most likely. Anyway," said Roger, "it shouldn't be difficult to settle that one. Ask her."

"I intend to," I said.

We got back about six and Uncle Arnold drove the car straight into the garage. The Mercedes wasn't here. I had a wash and a change and then went for a walk round the garden. I thought I might see Grizelda, but there wasn't any sign of her, and after half an hour of it I began to walk back to the house. I was just turning back into the courtyard when I saw Willi crossing it from the direction of the garages. On an impulse I stopped and watched him go into the house.

I gave him a couple of minutes and then, leaving the path, but walking as nonchalantly as I could in case anyone was watching, I made my way across a patch of open ground dotted with shrubs which brought me to the rear of the garages. The out-buildings themselves screened me from the house, but I spent a few moments pretending to admire the view and making sure there was no one else about. Then I turned my attention to the first garage.

There was a window about two feet square in the rear wall, but too high for me to see in; I could only just reach the sill with my outstretched fingers. I looked around and after a moment or two I spotted a fairish length of dead wood half buried in the soft ground. It was wet through but still sound and was well equipped with the jagged remains of branches. I propped it up against the wall and steadying myself by the sill, I managed to scramble up until my head was level with the lowest panes. But it was wasted effort; the gloom inside and the filthy state of the window made it impossible to see a thing.

I got down and was pulling the log away when I noticed that

the combined weight of myself and the wood against the slats that made up the wall had moved a section of slats about four feet high. The wood was rotten here and there and the nails had given way.

For fully a minute I stood there considering this unexpected development. I badly wanted to see inside that garage, but I had certainly no right to force an entry, and I should put Uncle Arnold in a very difficult position if I was caught doing so. Besides, it would be undignified, to say the least, to be hauled out by my ear like a common sneak-thief.

In the end, curiosity got the better of me and I eased the loose section back until I could get my head inside. There was an overpowering smell of damp and rust and oil, oil predominating, but I still couldn't see a thing. It was like putting your head inside an empty oil drum.

I couldn't understand it at first; even allowing for the grime on the windows there ought to be enough light coming in to relieve this complete darkness. I pushed the section back a bit more and a shaft of light fell on a solid wooden wall only two feet in front of me. I suddenly realised I was coming in immediately behind the bench on which Willi had been working.

My first feeling of disappointment gave way to a rising excitement. As long as I was careful to replace the loose slats I now had a perfect means of access to the garage whenever I chose; if there was a mystery, surely this was the way to clear it up.

Gently I eased back the section until its top end rested against the front of the bench. Then at the cost of a ricked neck and a couple of scratches I wriggled inside. I pushed the boards back into place, realising as I did so that the remaining nails were working loose. Much more to-ing and fro-ing and the whole thing would fall out.

But I was in. Clanking and clattering through the accumulated junk of years, I made my way towards a splash of greyish light at one end of the bench. I was about half-way there when I felt, rather than heard, the sliding door at the front being opened.

I lay still and listened to the rumble of its closing and then the echoing of heavy footsteps on the stone floor. They came up to the bench, paused, and then I heard the click of the light switch. Immediately a pattern of yellow slits sprang up along the front wall of the bench, and I realised that the whole length of it was served with little doors or hatches.

The next moment a hatch about three feet from my head was flung open and a shadowy arm and hand came groping in.

CHAPTER SIX

CURIOUSER AND CURIOUSER

OF COURSE I should have realised that with all the clutter of stuff there was under that bench that there must have been some way of getting it in and out. But it was no good telling myself that now—I could only keep my fingers crossed and hope that Holtz or Willi or whoever it was would find what he wanted straight away. There was a door slap in front of my face; he might just as easily have opened that one.

The hand moved about, roughly pushing things to right and left, and it became evident that this was not a search; a space was being cleared to take something fairly bulky. I began to breathe again.

The hand was withdrawn and I heard the footsteps again, clumping about at the far end of the bench. I tried to peer out through the cracks round the little door in front of me, but I could see only the shadowy outline of the garage entrance. With infinite care I lowered myself until I was lying flat on the stone floor, keeping company with the accumulated filth and oil and grease of years. How I was going to explain the state of my clothes I didn't know, but the main thing was that I could now see out through the open hatch, the door of which fortunately opened outwards.

It was Holtz all right, and he was folding back a heavy tarpaulin in the back of the little Volkswagen, which was parked against the wall. As I watched he lifted out a large, odd-shaped object which he carried over and stowed under the bench. I drew my head back into the deeper shadows as he leaned in, pushing the thing as far back as it would go, and then moving a random collection of odds and ends in front of it.

For a moment or two he sat back on his haunches, and then, apparently satisfied that the casual observer would see nothing unusual, he slammed the little door and I heard him go out of the garage. Five minutes later I was replacing my impromptu trap-door at the rear of the building.

Roger was in our room writing post-cards. I moved them out of his reach and made him listen to what I had to tell him.

"You know, you'll be getting yourself into trouble, young Jimmy," he said, when I'd finished. "A nice thing, for Uncle and me, to have you hauled off for breaking and entering. And just look at that suit. Almost new, isn't it?"

"Oh, dry up," I said rudely. I took off my jacket and trousers and slipped my dressing-gown on. I said, "I expect Hans can clean these things up a bit. Do you think you could manage to tell him if I go and have a bath?"

"I expect so," said Roger, reaching for his fountain pen. "Just press the bell as you go out, will you?"

"I was going to," I said, and did.

"Of course," said Roger, as I opened the door, "we might get Willi instead. If so, do you want me to tell him how you got them like that?"

I slammed the door.

A quarter of an hour later I was back again; the soothing hot water had done its work and I even felt able to cope with Roger's pigheadedness. But oddly enough he seemed much more reasonable, and I soon discovered why.

"Did Hans think he could do anything about those things of mine," I said.

"I didn't see Hans," said Roger slowly. "Frau Holtz said she'd do what she could."

"But I thought . . ."

"Yes, I know," said Roger. "But it seems Hans isn't here any more. I gather he's got the sack."

"The sack?"

"The sack. I asked her what he'd been up to, but as you know, her English isn't wonderful, and this evening it was even heavier going than usual. At first I got the impression he'd been pinching things—she certainly used the word 'thief.'

Afterwards she flatly denied she'd ever said it and claimed he'd been insolent to her husband. I couldn't make head or tail of it really. Then I said I thought Uncle would probably want to give him a tip and asked had he gone yet. That was the queer thing—she went as white as a sheet and couldn't get out of the room fast enough. Odd," said Roger reflectively. "Very odd."

I said, "Do I gather you're coming round to my way of thinking? That some people are up to no good?"

"At the moment I have an open mind," said Roger cautiously. "Tell me again about Holtz in the garage."

I ran over the facts again, stressing the pains Holtz had gone to in preparing his hiding-place, but I could see Roger wasn't convinced.

"It all seems so pointless," he said at length. "I agree it looks a bit eccentric to go hiding your old carpet sweepers, but maybe he just has a mania for tidying up. I expect it's broken."

"I didn't say it was a carpet sweeper," I said patiently. "I only said it looked like one. I didn't get a chance to see it closely, because he switched the light off before he went, but I felt all round it, and there weren't any brushes, or anything like that."

"Mm," said Roger doubtfully. "Could you draw it?"

"I'll try," I said.

I picked up Roger's pen and a sheet of writing-paper and did the best I could. "It's not very good," I said.

"No," said Roger. He looked at the sketch for a few moments with his head on one side, then he said, "No sign of any diving equipment, I suppose?"

I shook my head. "But of course I couldn't see very much. The helmet might have been still on the bench for all I know."

"I doubt it," said Roger. "Not if it *was* a diver's helmet. Well, I suppose we'd better go and chivvy Uncle to come and have dinner. You know, Jimmy, I don't think I'd say anything to him about all this. He can be a bit of an old fuss-pot, and I doubt if he'd quite approve of your recent activities."

He put the sheet of paper down on the desk and looked at it

speculatively for a moment. Then, "You know, it's a funny thing, but I can't help feeling . . ." He reached for his pen and drew a few swift strokes. "If it was more like this . . ."

He handed me the paper. "Yes," I said excitedly. "That's it. That's just how it looked. What is it, then?"

Roger took the paper from me and slipped it in the desk drawer. "That," he said, "is roughly what a mine detector looks like. Which makes the thing even more ludicrous."

We went in to collect Uncle Arnold and found him reading a letter. He waved it at us gaily and said, "Found a letter from Johnny Vermont waiting for me. Says he's running down to look us up on Saturday. I'm awfully glad he can manage it. You'll like Johnny."

After he'd read the letter out to us and told a couple of anecdotes about the war that Johnny Vermont's name had apparently recalled to him, Uncle Arnold began in his leisurely way to get ready for dinner.

"I'm afraid we shan't have Hans waiting on us this evening," said Roger.

"Oh! How's that?"

Roger told him. I walked over to the window with only half my mind on their conversation and stood looking out. A slight mist and the failing light had blotted out most of the view, and I could see little farther than the outer garden wall and the sweep of drive that led round to the garages. Suddenly I heard the hum of a car and the big, low Mercedes came in from the road. I watched it pass. Konrad was driving, and sitting in the back were the General and his niece, Grizelda. Well, I thought, it looks as though someone was speaking the truth. The General *was* only in a mood last evening and now he and Konrad have made it up. Perhaps, after all, there isn't any mystery. Just my imagination working overtime again. I turned away from the window telling myself to forget all about it and stop interfering in matters that weren't my concern.

Hans's place in the dining-room had been taken by a thick-set, red-faced man whom I vaguely remembered having seen doing kitchen work on the previous evening. He was as different from Hans as chalk from cheese. He was slow, rough-mannered, and wore a permanently bewildered expression; his clothes were about six sizes too big for him and his hands were none too clean. He appeared to answer to the name of Kurt.

We were again first in the dining-room and sat at the same table as the evening before, but we had barely started our soup when Konrad came in, very genial and hearty and flashing his smile in all directions. I was rather surprised to see him alone; I'd fully expected the Mercedes party to arrive together.

Uncle Arnold asked him to join us and he accepted effusively. He sat down next to me and leaned back in his chair, smiling round at all of us. Then he suddenly shot forward and announced with tremendous exuberance, "I am happy to say that all is arranged. We meet for the boar hunt at nine o'clock to-morrow morning. Transport, of course, we shall have to provide ourselves."

"Transport?" said Uncle Arnold. "Aren't we using the forest at the back here, then?"

"Not the Hochwald, no. It seems there is little or no sport to be had there. We go to another forest farther along the valley. They call it the Kallenwald. But you seem surprised, Major."

"Eh? No, it's just that . . . Never mind. What about guns?"

"Guns too. Holtz has two and has borrowed three more. They are . . ." he lowered his voice, "German Mausers. You will understand that it is better not to ask too many questions."

Uncle Arnold looked a bit put out at this. "I hope it's all right," he said.

Konrad dismissed his misgivings with an airy wave of the hand. "Pray don't alarm yourself, Major. A few of the farmers, you understand, have kept them as souvenirs. The authorities would naturally disapprove, but surely it is harmless enough. They are good fellows, all of them."

Uncle Arnold grunted uncertainly, but he didn't say any more and Konrad went on to tell us about the fun that was in store for us. If we'd known what we were really in for I doubt if we should have listened with such sheep-like docility.

It was in fact some twenty minutes before there was a turn in the conversation. Kurt had just served the sweet, and in doing so had spilled a small pool of raspberry sauce on the table. He cleaned it up in a messy sort of way, muttering a few awkward phrases of apology in German. He spoke no English.

After he'd gone Uncle Arnold said, "I must say I hope they manage to get a decent replacement for Hans before much longer. I suppose you heard he'd gone, Konrad?"

"Gone? Indeed, no. I assumed it must be his day off. But how surprising. What would cause Hans to wish to leave so suddenly?"

"I don't think he had much choice. As far as I can make out he was dismissed. At a moment's notice, what's more."

Konrad opened his eyes wide. "But that is extraordinary. What can the fellow have been up to?"

Uncle Arnold glanced at Roger and me. "I don't know," he said, and then after a pause added, "But I sincerely hope our coming here had nothing to do with it."

Konrad looked puzzled. "Surely not, Major. Why should it?"

There was another brief pause and then Uncle Arnold said briskly, "Exactly. Why should it?"

But Konrad was plainly determined to get to the bottom of it, and when Kurt came to clear away he addressed him in rapid German. I couldn't follow every word of their conversation because Konrad spoke with an accent and Kurt in a dialect of the country, but as far as I could make out it went like this:

"Where is Hans this evening, Kurt?"

"Hans is dismissed, mein Herr."

"Dismissed? Why is he dismissed?"

"I know nothing for certain, mein Herr. It is said Herr Holtz discovered that he had been stealing. My wife heard angry words and shouting in Herr Holtz's room. Hans tells us later that he is leaving. Very pale, he is, mein Herr. Very upset."

"But you know nothing for certain?"

"Nothing, mein Herr. Except that . . ."

"Except that Hans was shouting at Herr Holtz. Insolent, in fact?"

"Perhaps, mein Herr."

Konrad said no more and when Kurt had left us he said, "It seems Hans has been insolent to Holtz. Curious, isn't it, how little one knows people. Of course Holtz was perfectly right to send him away, but it is unfortunate. He was a good waiter, and I always found him courteous and honest."

"So did I," said Uncle Arnold.

After we'd had our coffee Roger and I left Uncle Arnold making final arrangements for the morning with Konrad and went back to our room. I was feeling puzzled and angry; puzzled because of the pattern of petty lies and intrigue that seemed to involve everyone at the Green Woodpecker, and angry with myself for being unable to ignore it and forget about it. As soon as Roger closed the door I burst out, "Konrad's in it too."

Roger looked at me in astonishment. "Eh?"

I said, "Asking Kurt about Hans. Kurt said quite definitely that there was talk that Hans had been pinching things. Why was he so careful not to repeat it to us?"

"Well," said Roger, "if it *is* only a rumour . . ."

"Rumour nothing," I said irritably. "You know jolly well there's something in it. And another thing. Why does Konrad wear a shoulder holster with a gun in it?"

"What?"

"His jacket was open and when he leaned across the table to give us his good news I saw it. Farmers with rifles are one thing, but you can't tell me Konrad is carting that thing round as a souvenir."

Roger didn't answer and I went over to my bed, where I could see my other suit lying neatly folded and pressed. I picked up the jacket and was beginning, "Well, she's certainly made a good job . . ." when I noticed an envelope which had fallen from between the folds. I opened it and read the few lines written in a firm, upright hand. I whistled and handed it to Roger. Wrinkling his brow, he read it back to me.

"Jimmy,—I am distraught with worry and can turn only to you for help. Will you meet me at ten o'clock in the summer-house by the west wall? Please, Jimmy. Grizelda.
"PS.: Hans will also be there."

"Well," said Roger, handing me back the letter. "Are you going?"

I looked at him in surprise. "Of course," I said.

"Yes," said Roger. "Yes, I thought you would." After a moment he added, "Getting quite the gallant knight, aren't you?"

He grinned as he said it, but I thought I detected a note of envy in his voice.

CHAPTER SEVEN

SECRETS IN A SUMMER-HOUSE

I LEFT the house by the little side door shortly before half past nine. Uncle Arnold was still hooked up with Konrad and I was saved the necessity of having to make explanation for going out. Roger said he'd cover up for me if need be.

It was a beautiful starlit night and there was a generous slice of moon as well. I knew I should have no difficulty in finding the summer-house, so I decided to walk round the garden for a bit. Inevitably I found myself being drawn towards the garages.

As I approached the first building I could see a chink of light shining under the sliding door. Making use of all the cover I could I picked my way through the sparse shrubbery and came up into the shadow of the rear wall. I decided it was too risky to attempt to move my loose slats with someone actually in the garage, but one corner of the section had sprung away and as I got my ear to the crack I heard a rumble of German. It was Holtz, and he sounded a bit keyed up.

"*Gott in Himmel*, will you hurry up? I'm twenty minutes late as it is."

There was a clanking sound, as if some heavy metal object was being dragged across the floor, and then Willi's voice, half aggressive, half whining.

"Well, it's not my fault. That fool of an Englishman wanted his boots cleaning. You should have . . ."

There was a sharp "clump," and Willi's voice broke off suddenly. I grinned to myself as I imagined him clutching his bullet head.

"Shut up," said Holtz. "And get this on your back. . . . Not that way, you fool; put your arm through here. . ."

There was a lot of straining and gasping, and then Willi's plaintive whine came floating back. "I'll never be able to carry this lot. Not all that way."

Holtz sounded furious. "You'll carry it. By all the devils, you'll carry it even if you have to crawl every step of the way. Now get those doors open. And get moving, before I have the hide off your back."

Willi must have taken him seriously because almost at once the building vibrated to the opening of the sliding door and immediately afterwards a car engine roared into life. I left my listening post and sprinted round to the angle of the wall from where I could see the Volkswagen as Holtz drove it out. In the glare of its headlights I had a momentary glimpse of Willi, a disconsolate figure weighed down under a huge pack, and carrying what looked like a carpet sweeper over his shoulder. Then the little car was careering down the long sweep of the drive and the garage and all about it was again in deep shadow. I heard Willi switch off the light, heard again the rumble of the sliding door, watched the dim outline of his passing until he was hidden by the second garage, and then listened to his receding footsteps as he trudged off in the direction of the forest.

I looked at the luminous dial of my watch. It was almost a quarter to ten. Dearly as I should have liked to know where Willi was headed for, there just wasn't time to find out if I was to keep my appointment with Grizelda. And what she had to tell me might well be equally important. Making sure there was no one else to see me I made my way round to the front of the house where the little rustic summer-house huddled in damp shelter of the west wall.

Grizelda was already there, but there was no sign of Hans. She spoke softly to me from the shadows. "Thank you for coming, Jimmy. You are very kind."

"Not at all," I said, a bit awkwardly. "I'd like to help, if I can, that's all. What's the trouble? Willi been making a nuisance of himself again?"

"No, no," she said. "Not Willi. Jimmy, will you come inside? They mustn't see us."

"The Holtzes?" She seemed to give a little shudder in the darkness. "Yes," she said.

I said, "Don't worry, they won't. Papa's off somewhere in

his car and the loathsome Willi's lugging about a ton of equipment into the forest. What's going on, Grizelda? What are they up to in the Hochwald at this time of night?"

"In the Hochwald?" She sounded puzzled. "I don't know. What makes you think . . ." She stopped suddenly and then went on, "Oh, you mean because of what Willi said to me this morning?"

"That—and other things."

"It is strange, certainly . . ." I waited for her to go on, but she didn't, and there was an uneasy silence for a moment or two. Then I said, "You mentioned that Hans would be coming. Is it about him you wanted to see me? Getting the sack, I mean."

"In a way, yes." She paused again and then went on in a rush. "Jimmy, I'm not asking for help for myself, or for Hans. I'm desperately worried about my uncle, the General. If things go on as they are I'm afraid he will—will do away with himself," she finished faintly.

"Good heavens," I said inadequately, and waited. Everywhere was very still; in the whole garden the only sound was Grizelda's quick breathing beside me. When she spoke again I could tell she was having difficulty in controlling her voice.

"My uncle is in some terrible trouble. It all began last summer when that man, that Konrad," she almost spat out the name, "came to our house in Berlin late one night and was with my uncle for two hours asking questions. I was not allowed to be present, of course, but I knew he was still there because eventually he called in two other men and together they searched the house. Some weeks later there was an inquiry, and my uncle resigned his post."

"Then Konrad is . . ."

"He is a security agent, although you would never guess."

"I agree. You never would."

"There is something else I must tell you. Hans was my uncle's servant for many years in Berlin. That must surprise you too."

"Well, not really," I said. "As a matter of fact we knew about it."

"You—knew?"

"Don't worry," I hastened to say. "Hans wasn't betraying any confidences. He had to tell us, really." And briefly I repeated Hans's story of the evening before.

When I'd finished, Grizelda said, "That is true. I too have treated Hans as a stranger all the time he has been here."

"But why, for goodness' sake?"

"Because my uncle wished it," she said simply.

"Yes, but . . . it's different for Hans. Surely you must have asked why."

"Once I did, when my uncle first told me. He said only that this way discipline would be better served. You must understand, Jimmy, that ever since we came here my uncle has been moody, preoccupied—I've known he had some great worry and felt it had to do with Holtz. When he told me he'd sent for Hans I thought, surely now things will be better, and gladly agreed to these conditions."

"And were they?"

"For a little while I thought so, a month maybe. But since then I've watched my uncle becoming more and more depressed, and now it's worse than ever before, for Konrad has come again to pester him with questions, questions."

"What sort of questions?"

"I don't know, they always talk in private. Like this afternoon. Konrad said my uncle must go with him to his office in Hanover and that I should go with them in the car, but hardly a word was spoken on the way and when we arrived in Hanover I was left to look round the shops for two hours. When we returned to find Hans had been dismissed and was already gone, I thought my uncle would break down. He . . ."

She sounded pretty near to tears herself. "It's all right," I said. "Take your time. Tell me when you're ready."

She sniffed a couple of times, swallowed, and then went on in a firmer voice. "I went to his room to see if he was ready for dinner. I knocked and went in, but he hadn't heard me. He was standing by the fire looking down at the Army pistol in his hand and he was as pale as death. He didn't know I was there until I ran across and took his arm. Then he gave a violent start and said he was just going to clean the pistol. But

I didn't believe him. I think he had reached such a state of despair that he might have taken his life. I made him sit down and tried to persuade him to confide in me but he wouldn't admit that anything was wrong. Why won't he tell me, Jimmy? I feel sure Hans is in his confidence. . ."

"If he is," I said, "it might explain a lot. Have you thought that Holtz might have some hold over your uncle?"

"Of course," she said. "I even asked him outright if it were so."

"What did he say?"

"Only that he paid Holtz to manage the hotel. Was it likely, he said, that he would employ a blackmailer?"

"Not very helpful," I said. I thought quickly. "Did you know that Kurt is under the impression that Hans was dismissed for stealing?"

She was highly indignant. "I'll never believe that."

"And yet," I said, "supposing Holtz is in possession of some letters or papers and is blackmailing your uncle, and supposing Hans broke into his room to try and recover them. . ."

For a moment she stared at me, her eyes wide. Then, "But no," she said quietly, "my uncle is not a man to permit servants to take such risks for him."

"Your uncle wasn't there," I reminded her. "And Hans seems to be pretty devoted to him."

"Oh, he is," she said passionately. "He is. He would die for my uncle, I'm sure. Jimmy, I believe you may be right in what you say. Poor Hans, he will be heartbroken that his desperate plan failed. . ."

I said, "It's just possible, of course, that it didn't."

"But surely . . . Holtz would never allow him to leave with this secret? He would have him searched, make him tell . . ."

"And if Hans had already hidden the evidence, and refused to say where? My bet is that he could be pretty stubborn. Holtz's main concern would be to get him out of the way before he was able to pass the stuff over to your uncle. Still, we don't know for sure and Hans is the only person who can tell us." I looked at my watch. "I suppose he *is* coming?"

"What time is it?"

"Ten-twenty. How did you come to arrange to meet him here?"

"I found a note waiting for me when we returned from Hanover. Just two lines, asking if I would be in the summer-house at ten o'clock."

"Did you tell your uncle?"

"No. I felt if Hans had wanted me to he would have said so."

"Yes." I thought hard. "It works both ways, of course. If Hans *was* after blackmail evidence and failed, he might feel he'd let your uncle down . . ." She didn't speak, but I knew she was staring intently at me in the darkness. "On the other hand," I went on, "if he *didn't* fail . . ."

"Yes?" she said eagerly.

"Well, it's pretty obvious your uncle's going to be watched day and night until Hans shows up. It would be asking for trouble to arrange a meeting with him. Chances are Holtz will be prying into your uncle's mail and even . . ." A sudden thought struck me. "That note from Hans. Where did you find it?"

"In the drawer of my dressing table. Why?"

"And you put it back there after you'd opened it?"

"I'm not sure. No, I think I may have left it on top of the dressing table. Jimmy, you don't think . . ."

"It's a bit early to think anything with so little to go on. But one thing sticks out a mile. Frau Holtz is as jumpy as a kitten where your uncle's concerned. She may not know all that's going on but I reckon she knows enough to make her frightened. And if Holtz is making her snoop round the bedrooms for information . . ." Another idea came to me. "That note you wrote me and slipped in the folds of my suit. . ."

"I—I don't understand," she said in a puzzled voice. "I just pushed it under your door."

Suddenly two bits of the jig-saw clicked into place. "Ssh," I said softly, and touched her arm. We listened to the stillness of the night, eerie, dead.

"It's getting late," I whispered at length. "Grizelda, I think we ought to be getting back. . ." I took her arm and steered her firmly on to the garden path.

"But Hans . . . if he should come . . ."

"I don't think he will now, do you? He probably decided it was too risky after all. Tell me, have you any idea where he's likely to be staying?"

"I think so. Schmelling, the baker in the village, used to be a close friend of his. I think he would go there."

"Right," I said. I glanced round. We were coming up on to the big lawn now and the summer-house was already hidden in the shadows. I lowered my voice. "We shall be coming back through Kallendorf after the boar hunt to-morrow. I'll make some excuse for dropping off there and try and have a word with Hans. I suppose you couldn't be there too?"

"I could try. What time will you . . ."

"It's difficult to say. Probably about six. I'll look out for you then. At the bakery?"

"I shall try to be there."

"Fine." I hesitated, then I said, "I suppose you don't think we might call at the police station and . . ."

"Oh no, Jimmy," she broke in vehemently. "Not the police. My uncle would never forgive me."

"I rather thought you'd feel that way about it." We had come on to the flagged path that led round the east wing of the house and as we turned the corner I detained her. "Just one more thing. Why did it give you such a shock when you first saw us sitting in the lounge yesterday?"

"A shock . . . to see you?"

"Yes," I said, a bit irritably. "You went tearing off as if you'd seen a ghost, you know you did."

She gurgled with laughter. "But Jimmy, don't you see . . ."

"Ssh." I gripped her arm and whispered, "Quiet." I edged back and peered at the lawn. The garden wall on the west side petered out just short of the rise to the house and in the dim glow from curtained windows I could just make out the outline of a man's figure coming from behind the wall and climbing the steps on the far side of the lawn.

"Golly," I breathed. The summer-house adjoined the wall and anyone on the other side of it could have heard every word we'd said. "You go on in," I told Grizelda. "To-morrow at six."

The man disappeared behind the west wall of the house and I slipped back on to the lawn and padded along to the farther flight of steps. Noiselessly I went up them and was just in time to see him walking into the courtyard. A light was burning in the kitchen and as he turned the angle of the wall I saw his face for the first time. It was Konrad.

I gave him a couple of minutes and then walked boldly round by the same route and in at the little side door.

Roger was in bed but still wide awake. He grinned at me as I came in. "Nice time to come in," he said. "What would Uncle say?"

"Did he ask for me?"

"Vaguely. I said I thought you were communing with Nature. Were you?"

"I was communing all right, if not exactly with Nature." And I told him all Grizelda had told me.

"Will you come along too, and help us interview Hans?" I asked him when I'd finished.

Roger looked at me speculatively. "Jimmy Keene, Special Agent," he said.

"Idiot. Well, how about it?"

"You want to know what I think? I think it's potty to get ourselves involved in this thing. Here's this General of yours, who's certainly been up to some sort of no good, blackmail or no, and a security bloke who's determined to pin something on him even if it means eavesdropping on your private conversations. Not very nice for you, I agree, but I expect it's all in the day's work for him. I don't see it gives us the right to interfere with the course of justice."

"I've no intention of interfering with the course of justice," I said hotly. "It's just that I want to . . ." I stopped suddenly, because to tell the truth, I hadn't much idea of what it was I did want to do. "All right," I said finally. "If you want to stay clear, stay clear."

Roger grinned again. "Now, now. Naughty temper. I never said I wanted to stay clear, I said it was asking for trouble. But I think it'd be asking for more trouble to let you go on your own."

"You'll come then?"

"I certainly shall. Together we shall do the Holtzes in the eye." He paused and then said, "Besides, there's one other little thing. You saw me put that little sketch in the drawer over there—you know, the thing that looked like a mine detector?"

"Yes."

"You didn't take it out again?"

"No. Why?"

"Have a look now."

I opened the drawer. There was a neat little pile of writing-paper and that was all.

CHAPTER EIGHT

THE BOAR HUNT

IT WAS about half an hour's run to the Kallenwald, and there were three car-loads of us. Holtz led the way in the little Volkswagen, with the oafish Willi beside him and Kurt and another man whom I later discovered was Kurt's brother Walter packed in behind. Then Uncle Arnold, Roger and I in the Daimler, with the Mercedes bringing up the rear, Konrad driving and the General riding in state on the back seat. I never really found out why the General came on the trip; I suppose it might have been just for the sport, but it seemed more likely that Konrad couldn't bear to let him out of his sight.

Konrad had suggested that we went with them in the Mercedes, but Uncle Arnold said he preferred to have his own transport with him, which was just as well in the light of what happened afterwards.

It appeared that Holtz had arranged with two of the local farmers to lend us a few of their chaps to act as beaters, and they were meeting us near the Kallenwald with the guns we were short of. There were to be six guns; Konrad, the General and Holtz, and Uncle, Roger and me. Kurt, Walter and Willi were to be extra beaters; I hoped sincerely Willi would get himself lost.

The men were waiting for us at a little farm on the fringe of the forest and we were invited to leave the cars in the yard. I could see Roger wasn't very keen on the idea—the thought of cows and things barging into the Daimler seemed to worry him far more than it did Uncle Arnold, but there wasn't much alternative so we locked up and stood around while Holtz proceeded to give the beaters their instructions. I could follow very little of what was said; they all spoke with a terribly strong dialect and half the time were shouting each other down, but the general drift seemed to be that for the morning at any

57

rate we would concentrate on the southern part of the forest where there was some measure of agreement the best was likely to be had.

Eventually we made a start, and by half past ten the dark green shadow of the Kallenwald enclosed us. It was very thickly forested, with a network of narrow rides criss-crossing it. I had a silly notion, as we marched in single file along one of these rides, that we must look like a firing party on a dreadful mission.

About three or four hundred yards inside the forest Holtz stopped and addressed us in English.

"Perhaps I may be permitted, gentlemen, to assign you to your positions. The beaters, as you will have seen, have entered the forest farther to the west, and will be working round in this direction." He indicated with a wide sweep of his arm. "The boar, if indeed there is a boar. . ." He waited a moment for the laugh, but it wasn't forthcoming. "The boar, gentlemen, in his endeavours to escape, will be rushing across these pathways, these rides, to gain safety in other parts. We must therefore place ourselves where we can see down these rides that bear off to our left here, and we must be very quick to shoot for he is not long in sight. One thing that is most important, gentlemen. There must be no shooting along the line of the guns, whatever happens. Should the boar, by some stupidity, run this way and cross this path, he must be left alone. Are there any questions, gentlemen?"

"What happens if I see a boar coming directly for me?" said Uncle Arnold, after a pause.

Holtz smiled. "That is most unlikely, Herr Major. But one thing more. Should you wound a boar, do not attempt to enter the forest after him alone. Please call for me and we shall then decide how it is to be done. Now to our positions. We cannot expect the beaters to approach for fifteen or twenty minutes, but it is as well to be ready."

The rides conjoined, sometimes as crossings, sometimes as T-junctions, at something like one hundred yard intervals. I found myself stationed at one of these intersections with Roger as my nearest neighbour and the General, whom I could just see if I stepped back into the line of trees, covering the ride on my other flank.

Everything was wonderfully quiet; the beaters, I decided, must be still a long way off and I should get ample warning of the approach of any boar. I sat down on a mound of grass and laid the rifle across my knees. Holtz had advised us to load before we separated—"put one up the spout," as Uncle Arnold called it—and I had five more rounds of ammunition in the magazine.

Half an hour passed, and nothing happened; it looked as if the beaters were making the dickens of a round trip of it. Now and again I waved to Roger and he gesticulated back, and occasionally I caught sight of Holtz, who had taken the ride beyond Roger, but the ride curved slightly and Uncle Arnold and Konrad, at the end of the line, were out of my line of vision.

Suddenly, and so unexpectedly that it made me jump a little, a shot rang out. I looked quickly to right and left; the General was standing exactly where I'd last seen him and didn't appear to have moved a muscle; Roger was looking away from me and craning his neck to see what was happening. After a few moments he turned and waved his hand to me in a negative way. A false alarm, I thought, and I was about to make myself comfortable again when his head flashed round and his whole body tensed in a listening attitude. A second later, and he whipped up the rifle and fired. I knew he'd missed, from the urgent way in which he brought the gun down and worked the bolt. He got it to his shoulder again but there was no second shot. As Holtz had predicted, the boar was not long in sight.

My heart was thumping as I waited for my chance; I strained my ears for the first sounds of the boar's approach. He had rather less than a hundred yards to cover—surely I must hear him any second now, crashing through the short, tangled undergrowth. I heard only a few faint, indistinct rustlings, such as a rabbit might make, or a small bird. I took a couple of paces forward and peered into the trees, and even then I nearly missed him.

He was standing quite still, head lowered, glaring at me with his little piggy eyes. A pair of wicked-looking tusks curved out from the foam-flecked jaws and stood out whitely against the grey carpet of pine needles. On his left flank was a bright splash of red. . .

I was so taken aback that for some seconds I just stood there gaping at him, then he gave vent to a nasty snuffling sound and began to move forward. He didn't charge, as I'd fully expected, but sort of waddled along, looking like a rather playful tank and about twice as menacing. Afraid to make too sudden a movement, I brought the rifle up to my shoulder in a deliberately slow movement, took careful aim and squeezed the trigger. Nothing happened.

Whether perhaps the boar had not seen me properly until that moment, I never knew; all I do know is that as I went on pulling at the trigger and getting more and more panicky, he suddenly stopped again, lifted his head and sniffed around, and then came on at a gallop.

He had less than the length of a cricket pitch to cover. For a split second I was tempted to run for it, but instinctively I knew it would be hopeless. I looked up, and saw the overhanging branch of a tree. I dropped the rifle and jumped.

I doubt if I could have done done it at any other time, but fear lent me, not so much wings, as the blades of a helicopter. I grasped the rough bark and hung on as the boar thundered by below me. I looked down, as well as I could, over my shoulder. He had stopped again and was sniffing the air in a definitely "I smell the blood of an Englishman" sort of way. Then he turned and came back.

I drew up my knees and shouted, "Help! Help!" as loud as I could. My voice came out all cracked and high-pitched. I hardly recognised it.

Faintly I heard voices shouting in answer, the faint thud of running feet. Then the General's voice, unmistakable, commanding. "Halt! Halt! *Gehen Sie mir aus dem Weg!*"

I could hear the boar directly underneath me, snorting horribly. I forced myself to look up and saw the General about fifty yards away, waving his arms to emphasise his demand for a clear field of fire. Uncle Arnold's voice came to me distantly. "Into the trees, Roger. He's going to shoot."

I knew I couldn't hold on much longer; why didn't he get on with it? I don't believe it even occurred to me that he might hit me instead. But the General had seen more firing ranges than even Uncle Arnold had ever dreamed of; he wasn't the type to take chances. What's more, he seemed to know better than I knew myself just how long I could stick it out. The shot came just as I was telling myself I was finished. I gritted my teeth and hung on for another ten seconds waiting for the second shot as the hulking creature threshed about beneath me. But it wasn't needed. I suddenly realised that it was all over, and my numbed fingers let go their hold. By the time Roger and the General came up all feeling of panic had passed and I was feeling thoroughly ashamed of myself.

I thanked the General in my best German with as much dignity as I could muster, and he smiled and patted me on the arm in quite an approving sort of way. I hardly dared to look at Roger. Uncle Arnold came puffing along, and it made me feel a good deal worse to see how shaken he looked; he hadn't been any too keen on my having a gun in the first place, and I felt I'd let him down badly.

"Sure you're all right, old man?" he said anxiously, as soon as he could get his breath. I assured him that I was as right as rain.

"How the deuce did it happen?" he demanded, looking from me to Roger, and then rather accusingly at the General, who had drawn back a few paces and was leaning impassively on his rifle.

I explained in a few words. "But I still don't really understand," I said. "I could have sworn I loaded the darned thing."

Roger picked up my gun and we watched him as he examined it. "Quite in order," he announced. "One up the spout as instructed." Then a broad grin spread over his face. "Only one little thing. You forgot to take off the safety catch."

I felt an absolute clot. Holtz and Konrad had joined us and at first were inclined to think the credit for bagging the boar should go to me. Uncle Arnold explained briefly, and without dwelling on my Tarzan act, for which I was very grateful. Then the beaters arrived, chattering excitedly amongst themselves and showering congratulations all round.

I was dreading the idea of Willi hearing the full story, and my ears were ready to catch the first sniggers, but Holtz merely told them that "mein General" had made the kill and then went straight on to the details of arranging transport for the carcass. Willi went off to get the Volkswagen and two of the beaters remained behind to help him load it. All the rest were then given fresh orders and went off happily to beat their way over new ground.

Holtz didn't waste any time; he got the guns moving again and we trekked off down the very ride that I'd been meant to cover. Uncle Arnold dropped back so that he was walking by my side and after a few moments he said awkwardly, "How about staying with me, old man, when we reach our new position? Bit lonely, isn't it, stuck out here by yourself?"

I felt myself flushing, but I knew he was worried stiff with the responsibility, so I swallowed my pride and said, "Yes, of course, Uncle. That'd be nice."

But the rest of the morning was a blank—the beaters didn't turn up so much as a rabbit. At one o'clock Willi drove up with the Volkswagen—and the picnic hampers. It was an odd sort of a meal, with social distinctions very strictly observed. Konrad sat with Uncle Arnold, Roger and me; Holtz was a little way apart, midway between us and the beaters; the General kept aloof, as always, and reclined in a half-standing position on a bank which, either by chance or design, was higher than any that the rest of us chose. From time to time one of the farm men would approach and inquire with tremendous deference whether he could perhaps bring him more food or another glass of wine.

For the afternoon session we moved to the eastern quarter of the forest. The method was always the same, and generally speaking we kept the same positions, except that as Uncle Arnold and I were sharing a post, the line of guns was relatively shorter.

At five o'clock Holtz announced the last shoot; Uncle Arnold and Konrad had both killed a boar and the day was reckoned to have been a great success, but we were all rather tired and it was getting chilly for standing about.

The forest was particularly dense in this part, and the rides were narrow, overgrown and apparently little used. I knew that Holtz was stationed only seventy or eighty yards to our left, with Roger and then the General beyond him, but for all we could see of them we might have been standing in the middle of the Black Forest. Konrad, at the end of the line on our right, was similarly veiled by the overhanging branches.

Sudddenly there was a shot, unusually loud because of the thick foliage, and for the same reason difficult to place.

"Where was that?" said Uncle Arnold. He brought up his rifle to the ready and I peered vainly through the trees.

"Might have been either side," I said, and took a few paces in Konrad's direction.

"Don't go far," warned Uncle Arnold, and then, "Listen!" he said abruptly. The sound was unmistakable, something was moving beyond the line of trees. "Keep back," he whispered, and herded me behind him with his left hand. "Wait for it . . ."

We waited for a few tense seconds, but no boar appeared. "Must have been farther away than we thought . . ." Uncle Arnold was saying, when another shot rang out and he fell in a crumpled heap on the ground.

CHAPTER NINE

ACCIDENT—OR DESIGN?

FOR A moment he lay there motionless and I stood aghast, powerless to move or speak. Then he groaned, rolled over on one side, and with an effort raised himself on to his elbow.

"It's my leg," he said. "My leg."

I pulled myself together and dropped on my knee, shouting, "Come here quickly. There's been an accident." Then, remembering the difficulty of identifying direction in that enclosed area, I added, "It's Major Keene. He's been shot."

Uncle Arnold was clutching the upper part of his thigh and his face was white with pain. There was a rent in his trousers and I tore this further until I could see the wound. It looked pretty nasty, blue at the edges, with a trickle of thick blood oozing from it.

They came running up, Roger, who plainly felt as helpless as I did, then Holtz and Konrad, who seemed interested only in holding an inquest.

"But what a dreadful thing," said Konrad, puffing and panting with exertion. And, "How did this happen?" demanded Holtz, looking from me to my forgotten rifle and back again.

"I don't know," I said shortly. "There were two shots, you must have heard them. The second one hit him. I don't know who fired them."

"I thought the Herr Major was shooting," said Holtz, and turned to Konrad, who nodded.

"Well, he wasn't," I said. "Look, is anyone going to help me with him?"

Just then the General came up, looking a bit blown, but no more so than Konrad. Immediately he took charge of the situation, and began issuing a stream of orders in rapid German. Whatever hold Holtz may have had over him in other directions, he gave way to him now, and went off bawling, "Willi, Willi," at the top of his voice.

Uncle was looking pretty grim but bearing up amazingly well. He didn't let out a sound as under the General's directions we made a rough splint for his leg and then constructed a makeshift stretcher, using a couple of stout branches and Roger's raincoat.

Holtz returned, having found Willi, and instructed him to bring the Volkswagen as near as possible to the scene of the accident. The ride was too narrow and overgrown to allow it to be brought right up.

We set off, Roger and Holtz carrying the stretcher, then Konrad and I, with the General stumping along behind. Konrad re-opened the inquest.

"Most unfortunate," he said to me. "Since neither Holtz nor I fired the shot, it seems as if your brother . . ." He shook his head sadly. "Most unfortunate," he said again.

Roger so far had scarcely spoken a word, and I'd reluctantly begun to come to the same conclusion, but I knew how rottenly he'd be feeling about it and discussing it with Konrad certainly wouldn't do any good, so I didn't answer. However, Roger overheard him. "I didn't fire at all," he said curtly. "I had no reason to."

Konrad flashed his teeth in a doubting smile. "But that is impossible. Holtz didn't fire, I certainly didn't, your brother has told us it was not he—that only leaves us with the General, and he . . ."

"Then it must have been the General, mustn't it?" said Roger, and turned his head as if the matter were settled.

"But the General would never shoot so wildly, and in any case was two hundred metres distant."

"You're not suggesting my brother's lying, are you?" I said coldly.

"But of course not. It's just that it is all so inexplicable. I will ask the General to make certain."

He dropped back and I caught up with Roger. "I was awfully glad to hear you say that," I said a bit awkwardly, "I was hoping it wasn't you, of course, but you hadn't said anything and . . ." I didn't quite know how to finish.

Roger didn't answer me directly. "The shot didn't come

S.F. C

from my side," he said definitely. "I'm quite sure of that."
He raised his voice a little. "What about the beaters, Holtz?"
Mightn't one of them have done it?"

Holtz answered without turning his head. "I do not see
how, Herr Keene. You must have seen for yourself that
none of them carried a rifle."

Roger said no more and after a few moments Konrad rejoined
us. "The General says it was not he," he said confidingly.
"As an officer and a gentleman I'm sure he wouldn't try to
evade the blame."

"No," said Roger. He looked down at Uncle Arnold, lying
with his eyes closed, his pallor startling against the dark blue
of the raincoat. "Anyway, I'm quite sure this isn't the time
to talk of blame, never mind try to fix it. Come on,
Holtz. *Schnell, schnell!*" It's the only German word he
knows.

Willi had brought the Volkswagen to an intersection about
six hundred yards away. He hovered around nervously as we
made Uncle Arnold as comfortable as we could, and all the time
there was an oddly worried look in his shifty eyes. There was
only room for one other passenger, and Uncle Arnold, who
had noticed that the General's gammy leg was giving him a bit
of trouble, asked that he should have the place. I took my hat
off to Uncle Arnold for that. He must have been in intense
pain himself.

Holtz got into the driving seat and swung the little truck
back on to the narrow, rutted track. I felt I could rely on the
General to see that he drove as carefully as possible. The rest
of us shouldered our rifles and trudged along in their wake.
There was a general feeling of gloom and despondency, and
nobody seemed inclined to talk, not even Konrad.

Willi led the way, and after a while I realised that Roger
was allowing him and Konrad to get on ahead. I'd been
putting in some heavy thinking myself, so I wasn't really surprised when he said in a low voice, "Just before the second shot
—I suppose Uncle *was* facing down his ride?"

"You're quite right," I said. "He was hit in the right leg.
It can't have come from your direction."

"So somebody's lying," said Roger thoughtfully. "Unless Holtz is wrong and it was one of the beaters after all. Of course, he might even be lying about that. . ."

"But why should he? After all, it was an accident. . ."

Roger's jaw tightened. "Was it?" he said.

I hadn't got quite as far as that. "You're not suggesting someone was trying to kill him?" I said incredulously.

"Keep your voice down. I'm not suggesting anything, only thinking aloud. Now, if someone had meant to kill him, he made a pretty fair hash of it, didn't he? And anyway, what reason could he have? Holtz, for instance?"

"If Hans was really trying to recover some blackmail documents, he might have threatened to go to Uncle when Holtz sacked him," I suggested.

"If Holtz is a blackmailer, he'd hardly want the police around, making inquiries. He couldn't have avoided it if Uncle had been killed, however much of an accident it might appear. Be your age, Jimmy."

"I suppose you're right. What about Konrad, then? After all, the boar hunt was his idea."

"Konrad *could* have done it, but why should he? Give me just one reason."

I thought for a moment, then I said, "It makes things difficult when you can't help liking the old General. . ."

"And his niece," put in Roger.

". . . in spite of the fact that he's supposed to have done something pretty shady, whereas Konrad . . ."

"You don't like Konrad? I'm not surprised. I don't, either."

I said, "I've nothing against him, really. He's a bit too oily, that's all. And I've an idea he'd stop at nothing to complete his case against the General."

"Even to eavesdropping on your private conversations with Grizelda?" said Roger with a grin. "Look out, he's at it again."

Konrad was indeed slowing his steps and letting us catch up with him.

"Willi tells me we are almost there," he said, addressing

Roger. "See, the farm is just in sight, through the trees."

"Good," said Roger. "The sooner we can get Uncle to bed and get a doctor to him the better I shall be pleased."

Konrad was silent for a moment, then he said, "Don't you think, Mr. Keene, that your uncle needs hospital treatment? I believe I could arrange for him to have a private ward, and as for you and your brother—well, hotel accommodation in Hanover is not difficult at this time of the year. . ." The teeth flashed apologetically. "Of course, it must mean your holiday is spoilt; for that I am truly sorry."

Roger didn't answer for a moment, then he said, "It's very good of you, Mr. Konrad, and of course we want to do whatever's best, but shall we wait and see what the doctor says? I don't suppose for a moment Uncle would want to go into hospital if it wasn't really necessary."

Konrad smiled again. "But who would? However, we shall see. I believe there is a doctor in Kallendorf. Holtz will know where he lives."

We were now coming down the slopes to the farm and nothing more was said. But Roger looked at me just once, and there was a strange look in his eyes.

They had made Uncle Arnold fairly comfortable in the back of the Daimler, and when we arrived Holtz had just finished paying off the men. They stood in a close group chattering in low voices among themselves. Holtz came a few steps to meet us.

"The Herr Major wishes you to drive his automobile," he said to Roger. "If you will be so good as to follow me I shall stop in Kallendorf at the house of Doktor Stein."

"Right," said Roger. "Don't go too fast, will you?"

"But naturally not, mein Herr."

Uncle Arnold was looking a little better, but although he didn't complain, he was obviously still in great pain. I didn't think he'd want to talk a lot, and since Roger was concentrating on avoiding every little bump in the road, we drove for the most part in silence. Only as we were coming within sight of

Kallendorf did Uncle speak of his wound, and what he said made me sit up sharp.

"Don't feel too badly about it, Roger, old man," he said. "I can tell you're worried stiff, but we all know it was a pure accident that could happen to anyone. I shall be on my feet again in no time."

"You—you don't think it was Roger?" I burst out.

Uncle Arnold looked dumbfounded. "Wasn't it? But Holtz said . . ."

"What did Holtz say?" said Roger, between his teeth.

"Well, I don't know that I can remember exactly, but I know I assumed . . . Something about your being inexperienced, and easily flustered—that sort of thing. But what made him say a thing like that, then?"

"What, indeed?" said Roger. "You know, Uncle, when we've got you safely back to the house I think we shall have to have a bit of a talk about friend Holtz. Eh, Jimmy?"

We came into Kallendorf. Half-way through the straggling village I caught sight of the bakery, but there was no sign of Grizelda. I looked at my watch: it was five past six. Something had obviously prevented her coming, but in the circumstances it was just as well.

We went on through the main part of the village and Holtz drew up in front of a big house on the outskirts. He jumped down and indicated to us that we should wait at the car before he ran up the steps and rang the bell.

He was only kept waiting a moment before an elderly woman answered the door and he was asked in. Three or four minutes later he reappeared and we saw that he and another man were coming out with a stretcher. It was only because I went to hold back the door for them that I caught a fragment of their conversation.

"My second emergency to-day, Herr Holtz," the doctor was saying, "and oddly enough both victims have had some connection with 'der Grun Specht.' Only this morning I was called to a place on the Hanover road where a poor wretch had been knocked down by some vehicle and left in the road. He was unknown to me, but the constable recognised him as a former servant of the General von Tarkenheim. Gruber, I believe they said his name was—Hans Gruber. Possibly he was on his way to seek re-employment, who knows?"

For a moment Holtz didn't reply, then he glanced at me, cleared his throat and said in a queerly hoarse voice, "Indeed I am shocked to hear this news, Herr Doktor. Gruber has in fact been working at 'der Grun Specht' for two or three months. How is the poor fellow?"

"There was nothing I could do for him, Herr Holtz," said the doctor. "He was quite dead."

We came up to the Daimler and Roger opened the rear door.

CHAPTER TEN

COUNCIL OF WAR

IT WAS half past eight and already dark when at last we turned up the gravel drive to The Green Woodpecker. Roger drove round to the rear of the house and brought the Daimler as close as possible to the little side door.

We got Uncle Arnold out of the car and with his arms round our shoulders the three of us shuffled through the narrow entrance. As we went in I saw the curtains move slightly at the last window in the east wing—I'd already decided that must be Grizelda's room.

We helped Uncle Arnold to his room without meeting anyone, but we'd barely got him settled comfortably before there was a knock on the door. "See who it is, will you, Jimmy?" said Uncle Arnold.

It was Frau Holtz; she was even paler than usual and I noticed a distinct tremor in her voice as she said, looking past me, "Herr Major, Holtz has just told me of your wound . . . this is so terrible."

"Oh, it's not as bad as all that, Frau Holtz," said Uncle Arnold. "Accidents will happen, you know." He was certainly looking a lot better and there was even an echo of the old heartiness.

"They should not happen so," said Frau Holtz, with surprising vehemence, then went on more quietly, "It is very painful, mein Herr?"

"Well, I won't deny it throbs a bit," said Uncle Arnold. "That medico of yours down in the village had to carve me about somewhat to get the bullet out. Still, I must say he seemed to know what he was about."

"The Herr Doktor has had much experience in these things. On the eastern front in 1945 he wins the Iron Cross."

"Did he now? Yes, I should say he's a good chap. What

was it he said, Jimmy? Ought to be on my feet again by Saturday?"

I said, "He thought Sunday. But he's calling to have a look at it on Saturday."

"Well, there you are, Saturday or Sunday. You know your husband wanted him to send me into hospital, Frau Holtz? I'm thankful he didn't manage to persuade the doctor."

She swallowed a couple of times, then she said, "My husband is very worried. He is anxious the best shall be done for the Herr Major."

"Of course, of course." Uncle Arnold smiled. "But I've had some experience of hospitals. All right getting in—not so easy getting out. Fortunately my nephews here backed me up. . ." He broke off and looked at his watch. "Good lord, you chaps must be famished. I hope you've kept them some dinner, Frau Holtz?"

"But naturally, Herr Major. Herr Konrad, he is just arrived in the dining-room."

"Good. Off you go then, you two. Perhaps I might have something here, Frau Holtz—only a snack, drop of soup and a poached egg or something."

"I see to it at once, Herr Major."

"Just a moment," Roger interrupted. "Why don't we stay here and keep Uncle company? That'd be all right, wouldn't it, Frau Holtz?"

She hesitated a fraction too long. "Of course," went on Roger smoothly. "I was forgetting you were so shorthanded. By the way, I suppose you heard the dreadful news about Hans?"

The remaining colour left her face and she swayed a little. I thought she was going to faint and took a step towards her, but with a visible effort she kept her feet, steadying herself by clutching at the door handle. There was a dead silence in the room as she tried to speak, but no words came.

"Must have been a dickens of a shock for you," said Uncle Arnold gently. "We were all frightfully sorry to hear about it. Only hope they catch the scoundrel responsible."

At last she found her voice, but it was strange and high-pitched. "What are they saying, then? Who—who are they seeking?"

"Why, the fellow who knocked him down," said Uncle Arnold in surprise. "Hit-and-run drivers—nothing too bad for them, in my opinion."

She said nothing, only nodding earnestly, and the frightened look was still in her eyes. " 'Course, I realise you must be pretty pushed," went on Uncle Arnold considerately. "I'll be all right, Roger. You and Jimmy go and have your dinner."

Frau Holtz seemed to pull herself together. "It shall be as you wish," she said unexpectedly. "The dinner shall be served in the Herr Major's room."

"But if it's going to put you out, Frau Holtz . . ."

"There is no trouble. I hope the Herr Major's wound will soon be less painful." And before any of us could say another word she was gone.

Driving up from the village I'd told the others how I'd learned of Hans's tragic death. Uncle Arnold was very cut up about it and seemed to expect that a big hue and cry would follow in which the driver of the vehicle responsible would be brought to justice. He was most indignant when I had to say that according to later fragments of conversation that passed between Doktor Stein and Holtz it appeared unlikely that the local police would spend a great deal of time on a case in which the driver was one in an unknown field of thousands and the victim merely a lonely little waiter without, as far as anyone knew, a relative in the world. Doktor Stein, in fact, was pretty cynical about the German police force altogether.

That was really about as far as we'd got in the car. But I felt, and I could tell Roger did too, that it was time Uncle Arnold knew more of the strange undercurrents that were swirling around us at The Green Woodpecker; of Grizelda's fears and suspicions, of Paul Konrad's persecution of the General, and the half-lies and insinuations that Holtz constantly let slip from under an unruffled cloak of civility.

It wasn't an easy story to tell, because there was no clear-cut mystery, only a collection of strange bits and pieces and a whole array of unexplained "why's." Roger didn't help matters; after telling me to go ahead and do the talking, he persisted in chiming in every few sentences until he got us all so muddled that Uncle Arnold said testily, "Look, it seems to me you might both have something to tell me, but so far it doesn't even begin to make sense. Could you perhaps come to some amicable agreement about the order of speaking?"

Roger grinned and said, "All right, Jimmy. The floor's yours." I took a deep breath and started again.

Ten minutes later Kurt came in with a dinner trolley. He'd made a quick change into his waiter's evening dress, but didn't seem to have had much time for washing. There was an uneasy silence while he fiddled about with cutlery and so on, and it wasn't until he was just about to go that Uncle Arnold said suddenly, "Just a moment, waiter—er—ober."

"Mein Herr?"

Uncle Arnold turned to me. "You were telling me how this fellow seemed to know more about Hans's dismissal than some people let on. How about trying him again?"

"You want me to ask him . . . ?"

"Well, first of all ask him if he's heard that Hans is dead."

It wasn't necessary. Kurt had picked up the name from our brief conversation and was wringing his grubby hands in what was evidently genuine distress.

"It is shocking, this news, mein Herr," he said to me. "For three months only have I known Hans Gruber, but already to me he was a good friend. I am most unhappy to learn how he is dead."

I translated. "Mm," said Uncle Arnold. "Ask him what he thinks Hans was doing on the Hanover road last night. Where he was making for."

Kurt shrugged and spread his hands. "How should I know, mein Herr? Hans never spoke of his personal affairs. Perhaps he decided to go back to his family—if he had one."

"Ask him why Hans left," said Uncle Arnold.

The moment I put this question Kurt's manner changed. His feet shifted and his eyes wandered from my face as he said awkwardly, "It is said he was insolent to Herr Holtz. That is all I know."

"Didn't Hans explain why he was leaving so suddenly?" I asked him, prompted by Uncle Arnold.

"Hans said nothing, mein Herr. If there will be nothing further . . ."

"Just one more," said Uncle Arnold. "Ask him if he remembers telling Konrad he believed Hans had been accused of stealing."

Before I had time to frame the question a slow flush began to spread over Kurt's face. He bent his head to hide it and didn't look up as he answered slowly, "I remember nothing of this. There is some mistake."

"I was there," I reminded him.

"With apologies, mein Herr, there must be a mistake," he said doggedly.

"Denies he ever said it," I reported.

Uncle Arnold nodded and looked speculatively at the wretched Kurt. "He's lying, of course, but we're not going to shake him," he said. Then briskly, "Let's not spoil a good dinner. Tell him he can go, Jimmy."

I told him.

Little was said over dinner; I don't think either Roger or I had realised how hungry we were, and Uncle Arnold, juggling with a tray and toying half-heartedly with his egg, asked no more questions as we got on with the serious business of eating. Eventually Kurt came in with the coffee; he looked pretty apprehensive and I thought rather surprised that he was allowed to go without further interrogation.

Only when Roger and I had quite finished and Uncle Arnold had got his pipe going did he say, "Council of War resumed. Now then, Jimmy, what else have you got to tell us?"

"I think I'd about finished," I said. "Sorry if it sounded bitty, but that's how it's been. I know you'll say all these things are open to quite simple explanations. . ."

"Not all," Roger put in.

"No, not all, but most of them. Before to-day, anyway. It's

not so easy to make them sound convincing when you talk about them—when they're happening it's quite different."

Uncle Arnold nodded. "Bound to make a stronger impression."

"Not only that," I said. "For example, I know this stuff about the General sounds a bit far-fetched, but I haven't any doubt that Grizelda's really terribly worried, and she meant it when she told me her uncle might take his own life."

Uncle Arnold puffed away for some moments without speaking. Then he took the pipe from his mouth, blew a cloud of smoke at the ceiling and said carefully, "I think we've got to tread rather warily here, Jimmy. You see, in the first place there's absolutely no evidence that Holtz is engaged in blackmail. On the other hand, it is a fact that General von Tarkenheim had to resign because he was concerned in some sort of shady dealings. If Konrad really is an accredited security agent, which seems very likely, and has instructions to complete a case against the General, I honestly don't see how we can possibly interfere, even if it is driving the old boy to the point of suicide."

"But, Uncle, we can't just sit back and let it happen," I said earnestly. "Don't you see, he probably saved my life to-day."

"I'm not forgetting that, Jimmy. And if there was anything else I could do to help him I would. But not this—we've no right to interfere with the course of justice."

"Just what I felt," said Roger.

"He's a soldier," said Uncle Arnold gently, "and he'll work things out in his own way. I don't think he'd thank us for butting in."

I couldn't answer. In a way I knew Uncle Arnold was right, but his words rang in my ears like a death knell.

Uncle Arnold turned on his elbow and pummelled and plumped up his pillows. "Well now, Roger," he said, when he was settled again, "what have you got to add to all this?"

Roger didn't answer at once; when he did speak he addressed himself as much to me as to Uncle Arnold. "To be quite frank," he said, "I can't get myself worked up into a state about the old General any more than you can, Uncle, though of course I do see Jimmy's point of view. Apart from that business this morning he's talked a lot with the niece, and a very nice-looking girl she is too." He grinned at me and I made a face at him.

"But there are one or two things," Roger went on, "that I don't care for. I don't care for young Willi's attitude, for one thing; I care even less for the idea that one of the hotel staff is rummaging among my private letters and . . ."

"Half a mo'," interrupted Uncle Arnold. "When did this happen?"

"Yesterday evening. Jimmy told you. Someone pinched that drawing I made. They must have been going through my letters to have found it."

"Ah, yes. The drawing of a mine detector. Now what the deuce would anyone want with that?"

"What would they want with a mine detector in the first place?" said Roger. "Not that I imagine it's a crime to own one. In fact, nothing that had happened to us until to-day was in the least the sort of thing you could go to the police about."

Uncle Arnold didn't say anything, just went on puffing at his pipe.

"I've given quite a bit of thought to this affair to-day," Roger said, rather self-consciously, "and this is the way I see it. Firstly, Holtz was determined to foist the blame for the accident on to me—now why? Well, he might have fired carelessly himself and been afraid to own up, but that isn't very likely, he's far too experienced. Or he might have been covering up for Willi—he was doing a lot of to-ing and fro-ing and could I suppose have sneaked a gun from somewhere—but from the way Holtz treats that lad I find it hard to believe. In any case, you'd expect a man in his position to be jolly careful before he tried to pin a thing like this on one of the hotel guests."

"But he must have realised you'd deny it if you hadn't fired," I said.

"Would you take Willi's word if the evidence was against him?" said Roger. "Holtz probably imagines that all boys are born liars and that parents and guardians treat them as such."

He turned back to Uncle Arnold. "Do you see now, Uncle, what I'm leading up to?"

"I'm not sure," said Uncle Arnold in a puzzled way. "But it seems to me you're making an incredibly serious accusation. Are you suggesting Holtz deliberately tried to murder me?"

"Not necessarily. Because there's a second point. I'm sure you'll agree that Holtz tried very hard to get you sent to hospital. If you'd gone to Hanover, Jimmy and I would naturally have gone too."

"You mean the whole thing was arranged . . ."

"To get rid of us. Yes, I think it was."

"But it's fantastic. And yet . . ."

"And yet not so fantastic if Holtz really has got something to hide and Jimmy's private eye stuff has got him rattled. After all, it'd be easy enough. He arranged the positions and this was a particularly winding path where people were out of sight of each other. He only had to creep up a bit closer along the fringe of trees, and he's a jolly good shot, we know that. Also, any other doctor but Stein would probably have bungled Uncle into hospital. That's something he overlooked."

"You seem very sure of all this," said Uncle Arnold.

"I am," said Roger confidently. "It seems to me it's the only way you can explain all the facts."

Uncle Arnold was silent for a few moments, then he said slowly, "Hans was sent away too."

"Yes," said Roger. "Maybe he knew something too, more than we do, in fact. Or maybe Jimmy's right and he actually managed to collar the blackmail evidence. Either way he was a danger to Holtz."

Uncle Arnold leaned over and deliberately tapped out his pipe into the ash-tray. "And Hans," he said softly, "was killed last night by an unknown vehicle on the Hanover road."

"Yes," said Roger again. "Remarkably convenient, wasn't it?"

CHAPTER ELEVEN

KONRAD SHOWS SOME IMAGINATION

WE TALKED the whole thing over and over again for about an hour. I could tell Uncle Arnold's leg was giving him a lot of pain and he was beginning to look very tired, but he wouldn't leave the subject alone until, as he said, we were all agreed on what the form was going to be. I think he was fairly convinced by Roger's arguments as far as the shooting incident was concerned, but as he pointed out, a police inquiry *might* only result in Willi or one of the other beaters being found to have loosed off carelessly with a borrowed gun, and certainly would entail a number of wretched farmers being prosecuted for being in possession of illegal firearms. Our own position in this respect wouldn't look any too good, either.

In the end Uncle Arnold said, "Look, I think the best thing will be for me to have a word with Konrad. He's not police, but as a security agent. . . ."

"But *is* he a security agent?" said Roger. "We've only got this girl's word for it, remember."

"I don't see any reason why she should lie about it," I began hotly.

"Calm down, Jimmy," said Uncle Arnold, and this time he spoke quite sharply. "There's no need to get quite so hot under the collar. Roger's quite right, and before I took Konrad into my confidence at all naturally I should want to see his credentials."

There were a dozen reasons I wanted to put forward to oppose this particular course of action, but I couldn't be sure how much I was influenced by what Grizelda had told me, so I said nothing.

"Konrad arranged for the borrowed rifles," Uncle Arnold went on, "so a police inquiry would embarrass him even more than us. On the other hand, he might know a bit about friend

Holtz, and I feel sure he'd be as anxious as we are to find out who fired that shot, and why."

I found myself remembering the walk back from the Kallenwald, and Konrad's scepticism when Roger denied responsibility, but Roger made no comment. There was rather a long pause.

"Well, that's settled then," Uncle Arnold said at length. He turned to me. "Jimmy, I'm not going to ask you not to see this girl—what's her name, Grizelda—but I do want you to be careful not to get yourself mixed up in her uncle's affairs. There may be all sorts of things involved—you know, politics and so on—and we've certainly no right to make things more difficult for the authorities than they probably are already in a delicate business of this sort. All right?"

"You want me to promise . . ." I began doubtfully.

"I'm not asking you to promise anything," said Uncle Arnold. "I think you've got the sense to see what harm you might do by meddling in a thing like this. And another thing. There have been two accidents already which may not have been as accidental as they appeared. We don't want any more. Just bear in mind that I'm responsible for seeing that you both get home in one piece and don't go asking for trouble."

He looked very severe as he said this and we grinned back rather sheepishly. "I'll put Jimmy on a lead, Uncle," Roger said.

"Maybe you'd better, at that. Right, well I'm going to get some sleep now, if this confounded leg will let me. Put the light out as you go out, will you?"

I looked at my watch as we came out of Uncle Arnold's room. It was five minutes to ten.

I said, "I don't think I could sleep yet. How about a walk round the garden?"

"Whither thou goest, there go I," said Roger. We went out by the little side door and turned towards the front drive.

After a few moments Roger said, "Where's this summer-house of yours?"

"More or less the way we're going," I said, as casually as I could.

"I thought it might be."

We didn't talk any more as we crossed the big lawn and passed into the leafy shadows beyond. Here and there a shaft of moonlight pierced the trees and one luminous finger pointed directly at the doorway of the summer-house. Framed in the doorway stood Grizelda.

"Oho!" murmured Roger.

"Shut up, you idiot."

She greeted us with her shy smile as we came up, but I could tell she'd been crying. "I thought you might come," she said softly.

"It was ten o'clock," I said, by way of explanation. "When you weren't in the village this evening I wondered whether..."

"You knew about..." She stopped.

"About Hans? Yes. I'm—we're terribly sorry. Grizelda. How—how did you hear of it?"

"Frau Müller—Kurt Müller's wife—was in the village this afternoon, shopping. She brought the news. It was—oh, it was dreadful."

"Of course," I said. "It was a shock to us too. How did the General take it?"

She didn't answer at once. Then she said, haltingly, "My uncle has not been told. I—I couldn't tell him, Jimmy."

I suppose we were both a bit taken aback. "But surely you can't keep it from him indefinitely," Roger said after a pause. "I mean, someone's bound to tell him sooner or later."

She said earnestly, "He mustn't know yet. Not while he is feeling like this—so depressed, so wretched. I think it might ..." She caught her breath and I could see she was struggling to keep back the tears. After a moment she went on more calmly, "I have asked Frau Holtz and the Müllers to say nothing. I think they will respect my wishes. I do not believe Holtz will speak of it either."

"Even so," said Roger, "almost anyone in the village might mention it. It must be common talk down there."

"My uncle very rarely leaves the house and I can't remember when last he went into Kallendorf. There is no danger there."

"Aren't you forgetting someone?" I said. "Konrad?"

"Yes. There is Konrad. I had not forgotten. But would Konrad—is it likely he would listen to me? I believe he hates me as he hates my uncle. That's why I wanted to see you to-night, Jimmy. I wondered if perhaps Major Keene . . ."

"Speak to him, you mean?" I glanced at Roger and almost imperceptibly he shook his head. "It's rather awkward, you see, Grizelda. . ."

"I'll speak to him," said Roger unexpectedly.

I looked at him in amazement. Blandly he went on, "After all, it's fair enough. Quite see your point, Fraulein. There's absolutely no call to distress your uncle any further. I'm sure Konrad will see that."

Again the warm, shy smile. "Please, it's Grizelda. Thank you both, so very much. I feel happier now."

There was a little pause and then I said, "I suppose you heard about Uncle Arnold—Major Keene's accident?"

She looked bewildered. "No. No, I heard nothing."

"This afternoon," I said, "during the boar hunt." And I told her the facts, as briefly as possible, and without mentioning our own theories about how it happened.

"This is so strange," she said. "My uncle told me nothing when he came home, although I tried to make him tell me about the hunt. Of course, I saw no one else—for the past hour I have been walking round the garden. Oh, Jimmy, here I am, burdening you with my troubles, when. . ."

"He'll be up in a couple of days," said Roger, "and there's nothing we can do for him until then, so it leaves us at rather a loose end. At your service, ma'am, if there's anything else at all we can do to help."

She hesitated for a moment, then she said, "You have been so good, I don't like to ask any more. . ."

"Nonsense," said Roger briskly. "Out with it."

For a moment she bit her lip in indecision, then she gave a little smile and said, "It's about Hans. Perhaps the police may find his family, I don't know. Perhaps they won't trouble. But I should like him to have a decent burial, and I thought . . ." She held out a thick envelope. "Could you take this money

to Schmelling, the baker, and ask him to make the arrangements? You could say it was the wish of—of a friend."

I took the envelope and put it in my breast pocket. "Of
course," I said. "We'll go first thing in the morning. Anything
else?"

"Nothing. You have done too much already. I must go
now. Perhaps you will let me know. . ."

"After lunch, to-morrow," said Roger. "We'll just happen
to be strolling in the garden."

She nodded, smiled, and was gone.

I looked at Roger and he grinned sheepishly back. "Who
was it," I said, "who had the nerve to talk about gallant
knights?"

When we went in to see Uncle Arnold about eight the next
morning we found him hobbling round the room on a stick
and muttering under his breath at the pain. It took us five
minutes to persuade him to get back into bed and another ten
to make him promise to stay there. And then only after we
undertook to call on Doktor Stein whilst we were in the village
and try to get him to come up to the hotel later in the day.

As we were leaving to go for breakfast Uncle Arnold said,
"Oh, and if you should see Konrad, ask him if he'd be good
enough to drop in for a chat, will you?"

Outside the door I asked Roger if he'd decided how he'd
make his appeal to Konrad. "Not really," said Roger. "I'm
going to wait and see what he says, first."

The dining-room was empty, except for Kurt, who had
evidently dressed in a hurry and spent even less time on shaving.
Konrad came in as we were drinking our second cup of coffee.
He flashed his teeth whitely and gave us a hearty good morning.

"Good morning, Herr Konrad," said Roger smoothly.
"We've about finished, but if you'd care to join us . . ."

Konrad gushed in his usual way and sat down at our table,
immediately inquiring after Uncle Arnold.

"He's not a very good patient, I'm afraid," said Roger.
"We're having a bit of trouble with him—for some reason or
other he just hates bed."

Konrad looked most concerned. "But the Major must rest

until his wound is mended. Doktor Stein was most specific on this point."

"That's what we've been telling him," said Roger. "Don't worry. I think he'll be a good boy now. But it's a bit boring for him, you know, especially if Jimmy and I are going to be out."

"You are going out this morning? Then I shall myself entertain the Major. You think he would like that?"

"I'm sure he would," said Roger encouragingly.

Just then Kurt arrived with a fresh lot of coffee and took Konrad's order.

"Disgusting creature," said Konrad, wrinkling his nose at Kurt's retreating back.

Roger nodded agreement. "Not a patch on poor old Hans."

Konrad crumbled a roll. "You heard, I suppose," he said, looking from one to the other of us.

"Only the bare facts," said Roger. "No details."

Konrad shrugged and bared his teeth. "But what details could there be? Hans is walking the long road to Hanover, clutching his pathetic little attaché-case. Suddenly there is a blaze of lights and some criminal fool sweeps round a bend at one hundred and twenty kilometres per hour. No time to swerve, no time for Hans to jump. Croomp!" Konrad clamped his palm hard against his other fist. "There. All over in one fraction of a second. The motorist panics and drives on. Perhaps the car is damaged; if so he will get it repaired at some obscure garage miles from the scene of the accident. There were no witnesses—he is safe."

"You think that's how it happened?" said Roger.

Konrad shrugged again. "Very likely. Who can say? Who will ever know for certain?"

"Were his injuries very bad?" I asked him.

Konrad turned to me, his eyebrows lifted. "He is dead. One must assume that they were. I have no information." Still addressing me, he went on, "It's most unfortunate that this news reached the hotel during our absence yesterday. It will be most distressing for our host, the General."

Roger stirred slightly beside me but neither of us answered, and Konrad continued, "Doubtless Fraulein Grizelda will have told the General by this time, and doubtless she will have done so as gently as possible. With people in a highly nervous state that is most important."

"She may not have done so, of course," I said after a pause.

Konrad nodded slowly. "I would suggest to her that it was unnecessary to say anything, but alas," the teeth flashed disarmingly, "the fraulein and I are not on very good terms." And he went on looking at me.

I nodded understandingly. "Perhaps I might drop a hint to her," I said.

"You might do that, my friend," said Konrad, a shade too casually. "But after all, it is not really our concern. One tries to be understanding, that's all."

Kurt approached with a tray and Roger and I got up. "We'll tell Uncle Arnold you'll be popping in to see him then," said Roger.

"Indeed, yes. I look forward to a most pleasurable conversation."

We left him to his plate of sausages.

We went in to tell Uncle Arnold we were going and that Konrad would be dropping in to cheer him up.

"Don't forget to go and see the doc., that's all," said Uncle Arnold, pointing a warning finger at us. "Want to take the car?"

"Thanks very much, Uncle," said Roger without hesitation. Driving's been a mania with him, ever since he got his licence, and of course the Daimler *was* rather special. "Rely on us. If necessary we'll drag him here by his stethoscope."

As we crossed the courtyard Roger said, "Wonderful imagination, that chap Konrad. About Hans, you know. Described the accident as if he'd been there watching it."

"Mm. P'raps it's just as well then that I can vouch for it that he wasn't," I said.

"How's that?"

"Because Doktor Stein happened to mention that he put the time of Hans's death at between ten and eleven o'clock last night. Between ten and half past Konrad was too busy eavesdropping on Grizelda and me to be even thinking of Hans, and if he'd gone out within the next half an hour or so I think we should have heard the car."

"Oh, I don't know. . ."

"On the other hand," I went on, "Holtz *did* go out in that little truck of his, some time before ten. I told you, remember?"

"You're quite right," said Roger. "I heard it, now I come to think of it. Yes, that does seem to let the Merc. out. She's got a roar like a jungle tiger."

We came up to the garages. The door of the first one was shut as usual, but from inside there came the sound of hammering.

"Willi's at it again," said Roger. "What's your guess? Straightening something out?"

"Such as?"

"Oh, I don't know. Bumper bar? Wing?"

"Aren't we rather jumping to conclusions?" I said.

" 'Course we are. But they're interesting, don't you think? I'd love to get a squint in there."

"There's the way in from the back," I said doubtfully. "But . . ."

"Hardly. Not in broad daylight. But we'll bear it in mind."

We pulled back the door of the second garage. Roger walked round the Mercedes, paying particular attention to the front. "Not a scratch," he reported. "And he certainly hasn't had time to have her re-sprayed. Oh well, come on."

"Half a tick," I said. "What do you make of this?"

The folded sheet of stiff paper had been lying half under the Mercedes, on the driver's side. I opened it out more fully and spread it on the bonnet.

"It's a large-scale map," said Roger. "Forest, mostly, by the look of it."

"It's the Hochwald," I said, and indicated the titling.

"So it is." Roger stared at it for a second or two, then reaching out to point he said, "Odd, that bit there. You'd hardly expect . . ."

"Excuse me, meine Herren," said a voice behind us. We spun round.

Holtz smiled ingratiatingly. "I see you have found Herr Konrad's map. He has searched everywhere for it. You will permit that I restore it to him?" His long arm stretched out between us.

"A map Herr Konrad uses for the sport," said Holtz, deftly folding it. "He would have been sorry to have lost it."

He smiled again, turned on his heel and walked off briskly in the direction of the house.

CHAPTER TWELVE

THE BAKER OF KALLENDORF

WE DROVE half-way to Kallendorf in silence, each busy with his own thoughts. Then Roger said suddenly, "Didn't Konrad tell us they didn't hold boar hunts in the Hochwald?"

"He did."

"Mm. I thought so. Then what would he want with a large scale map of the forest? Any ideas?"

I said, "It probably isn't Konrad's at all. Holtz is the one with an interest in the Hochwald. Remember, he sends Willi on little errands?"

"You're right, Jimmy! Golly, you're right. Then perhaps that odd . . ." Roger broke off, swung round and clapped me painfully on the leg. "The diving helmet! How about that, then?"

I nodded. "It's beginning to hang together," I said.

We came into Kallendorf and parked the Daimler in a little open space by the village pump.

"What now?" said Roger. "Doctor first, or baker?"

"We might have a look at the surgery hours," I said. "Then at least we'll know when to find the doctor in."

Surgery hours turned out to be nine-thirty to eleven. The outer door stood open so we went in and took a peek inside the waiting-room. Although it was only just after half past nine the place was already full of people, all of whom stopped talking and stared at us with frank curiosity. We withdrew in some confusion.

"Unhealthy lot around here," was Roger's comment. "Try again later, eh?"

We found the baker, Schmelling, at breakfast. He was a big man, though rather on the flabby side, with a completely bald head and a face the colour of his own dough. Still chewing, he opened the door to us himself, and although I said we could easily call again later, insisted on our going in and with much ceremony ushered us into the best room, where there was a thin film of dust over everything and an overpowering smell of mothballs.

Apologising for his shirt sleeves, the state of the house, and the lateness of his breakfast time—apparently the poor man had been up since four, baking—Schmelling excused himself and reappeared a couple of minutes later wearing a dark jacket which merely emphasised the fact that he wasn't wearing a collar. Still, it seemed to put him more at his ease, and after flicking at the two best chairs with a large red-spotted handkerchief he got us seated and expressed himself entirely at our disposal.

I'd got my opening speech, in what I hoped was faultless German, already prepared. "First, Herr Schmelling," I said, "we should like to express our condolences on the death of Hans Gruber, whom we understand was a friend of yours."

The big moon-face was very grave and I'll swear there were tears in his eyes as he said, "Indeed it is true, mein Herr. Hans was my very good friend for many years. It is terrible that after so long I see him for such a short time and then—this."

"Such a short time?" I repeated."

"Four hours, mein Herr. And so much to say to each other. In four hours we had scarcely begun."

"You didn't know then, that he'd come back to 'der Grun Specht'?"

At once his expression changed and the pale blue eyes were veiled with suspicion. "May I ask where you come from, mein Herr?"

"As a matter of fact, we're staying there ourselves . . ."

"Ah!"

". . . but we are no friends of Holtz. Please believe that."

For a moment or two he weighed us up, saying nothing. Then, "You are British?"

I nodded. "We are on holiday with our uncle, who was a major in the British Army."

That seemed to clinch it. The doubts faded and Schmelling began to talk. I think he was glad to get it off his chest.

"Hans came to me on Wednesday afternoon. I was over-joyed to see him but I quickly realised he was in great distress. For a long time he would tell me nothing of his trouble, except to say that he could stay only a short time—that he must leave after dark. I pressed him to stay the night, at least, but he insisted it was impossible. I begged him to let me share his trouble—there must be some way in which I could help, I said. In the end he told me a little—perhaps he thought enough to satisfy my curiosity, though I swear to you, mein Herr, my only thought was to help Hans."

I nodded again. Roger was looking thoroughly fed up. This was obviously all very interesting and he wasn't getting a word of it.

"Of course we knew in the village that the Herr General was back in residence, but it came as a great shock to me to learn that Hans was here, too, for several months past. At first I was hurt that he had not been to see me, but Hans explained that the Herr General did not wish Holtz to know that Hans had been his servant. If Hans had been seen in the village Holtz might have learned of this.

"Of his dismissal Hans was reluctant to speak, except to assure me that he had done nothing dishonourable. But of course I should have known this anyway. All the same, I felt he was afraid of something. As he told me of these things he was all the time glancing over his shoulder, starting at the slightest sound. At the evening meal he ate practically nothing.

"At nine o'clock precisely he left my house. Nothing I could say would induce him to stay a moment longer."

He took out the red-spotted handkerchief again and una-shamedly wiped his eyes.

"Our deepest sympathy, Herr Schmelling," I said awk-wardly. "It must have come as a dreadful shock to you to learn of the accident."

He transferred the handkerchief to his nose and trumpeted into it several times before he said. "It was Frau Jaeger, the Herr Doktor's housekeeper, who told me. She used to keep house for old Doktor Schmidt, in the good days before the war, and she knew of my friendship with Hans. It was kind of her to think of me."

I agreed. "I suppose a lot of people in the village would remember him," I suggested. "Even," I went on casually, "if he wasn't carrying documents of identity."

"It is strange you should say that, mein Herr. According to Frau Jaeger they found no documents of any kind on the—the body. Even the attaché-case seems to have disappeared."

"The attaché-case?"

"Yes, mein Herr. Hans arrived with one large suitcase, but he asked if he might borrow something smaller, as he wished to take only a few belongings and might have a long walk ahead of him."

"So when he left . . . ?"

"When he left he had only a small attaché-case which had been my wife's."

I said to Roger, "Hans left here carrying one small attaché-case. When they found him there was no sign of it. Chew that over for a bit."

Roger's eyebrows went up but he didn't say anything. Turning back to Schmelling I said, "I hope you will forgive all these questions, Herr Schmelling. The fact is, we are here at the request of another friend of Hans, who wishes to be sure that proper arrangements for a decent funeral are made." I took the envelope out of my pocket and offered it to him. He didn't take it at once, but said eagerly, "From the Herr General?"

"I'm not at liberty to mention names," I said, "but not the Herr General, no."

He hesitated. "May I ask—is this friend a young lady?"

I looked at Roger, but I wasn't going to get any help there. The whole conversation had gone clean over his head. "Yes," I said at length. "It is a young lady."

Schmelling beamed at me. "Then I shall accept the money and poor Hans shall have a good funeral. I had planned to reserve for myself the honour of paying for it, but . . ." He broke off and looked at me oddly for a moment or two. Then he seemed to come to a decision.

"I shall tell you everything," he said. "Just before Hans left he came to me with a certain book and said to me, 'Old friend, they will ruin my master if they can. Take this, and if anything happens to me, see that the Herr General has it. But,' he said, 'do not, above all, let it fall into Holtz's hands.' I believe," went on Schmelling, "that you, meine Herren, would not see harm come to the Herr General, and I will therefore ask if you will be so good as to deliver it safely to him."

He rose, apparently taking our agreement for granted. Roger nodded in a vague sort of way and I wasn't really left with any alternative. "Of course," I said. "With pleasure."

Schmelling went out of the room and I took the opportunity of giving Roger the gist of these confidences. Roger looked very thoughtful. "If anything happens to me," he repeated. "The poor old thing could hardly have expected to be knocked down by a motor car, could he? Jimmy, old son, I'm beginning to think we've no right to keep this lot to ourselves. Another little talk with Uncle is indicated."

Schmelling came back with a large book in his hand. The moment he got into the room he went off into an agitated torrent of German.

"Now what's up?" said Roger.

"He says he's just been in the little box-room where he put the rest of Hans's things. He says somebody's broken into the room and turned everything upside down."

Roger nodded at the book. "That what they were after?"

"He seems to think so," I said. The baker was already explaining to me that nothing had apparently been taken, and how thankful he was that he had put the book away in his own bedroom.

"Well, there it is, then," said Roger. "Here's a solution that lets us out. He must go to the police and report this, and while he's about it he can say that Hans actually seemed to be in fear of his life."

"Mentioning Holtz by name?"

"That's up to him. I think he ought to tell them everything he knows."

I put this to Schmelling. He nodded slowly all the time I was talking, looking from one to the other of us with big, round eyes. He was a simple soul, but I felt utterly honest and loyal to the last.

"You are right, mein Herr. I shall go to the constable and report this burglary. Also I shall speak of Hans's fears. But not of the book—that is not my secret. You will put it into the Herr General's hands, mein Herr?"

He held out the book and as I took it from him I realised what it was. An old-fashioned, leather-bound snapshot album.

We found an old newspaper in the Daimler and wrapped the album in it. "Notice the low cunning," said Roger. "People will merely think we're carting a packet of fish and chips around with us."

There was only one person left in Doktor Stein's waiting-room, an old man of about a hundred and three. We sat for about four or five minutes and then the doctor himself opened the door. He was about to call Methuselah when he noticed Roger and me. "What's this?" he said briskly. "More patients from 'der Grun Specht'?"

We got up. "No, Herr Doktor," I said a little nervously. "It is just that my uncle, the Major, is anxious to be about again. He wondered if you could possibly come to-day to examine his wound. He—he seems to think it is almost healed."

Doktor Stein grunted. "Doesn't like bed, eh? Well, then, he shouldn't go fooling about with rifles. I'm a busy man, young fellow. Does he think I've nothing better to do than run about after a bunch of careless sportsmen?"

"I—I'm very sorry, Herr Doktor," I stammered. "But you see . . ."

"I know, you were just delivering a message. Is that it?"

"Well—er . . ."

"I understand. Well, take one back. Tell this uncle of yours, this Major, that if he wants to spend three months in hospital he can get up and run about after more wild boar. If he wishes to return to England next week he had better stay where he is until I see him. I shall come to-morrow evening at six. Understood?"

"Of course, Herr Doktor."

"Good." He turned to the old man. "Schultz!" he barked. The old man awoke from a half doze. Doktor Stein crooked his fingers and strode out of the waiting-room. The old man shuffled after him.

On the step Roger said, "Well, what time is he coming?"

I'm afraid I bit his head off.

CHAPTER THIRTEEN

THE SECRET OF THE ALBUM

AFTER A good bit of discussion on the way home we decided to say nothing to Uncle Arnold of our conversation with the baker. It would be impossible to speak of it without explaining our reason for going to see him in the first place, and mention of Grizelda would immediately set him off again about interference in matters that didn't concern us. In any case, he was probably going to hit the roof when he got Doktor Stein's message, however tactfully it was put.

It was almost twelve when we put the Daimler away. The other garage was shut up, as always, but quiet. As we walked towards the house we saw Willi chopping wood by the kitchen door. He watched us all the way as we crossed the courtyard.

"He'll be off like a shot the moment we're out of sight," said Roger, "reporting a strange parcel wrapped in newspaper. We'll have to find a jolly safe place for it."

"Can't we take it straight along and hand it over to the General?"

"Hardly. At the moment Holtz can't be sure it isn't fish and chips. But I reckon he's keen enough to get this back to go the limit once he *is* sure. And if we were seen handing it over to the General . . . I hate violence," said Roger fastidiously. "We'll hang on to it until after lunch and then let Grizelda take charge of it. It's just a question of where to put it in the meantime."

We tried several hiding-places in our room, under the wardrobe, behind the chest of drawers, even in the chimney, but none of them seemed good enough. Eventually Roger hit on the bright idea of covering the album in brown paper to match a couple of engineering books which for some reason he'd brought with him. We then left all three books in a casual pile on the bedside table, the album in the middle.

We found Uncle Arnold distinctly peevish, and as I'd

expected, it didn't help in the least when we had to tell him he couldn't hope to see the doctor again until the following evening. We tactfully let him blow off steam for a while and then Roger asked if Konrad had been to see him yet.

Yes, Konrad had been in. He'd had a long talk, a very interesting talk with Konrad. Konrad had shown him his credentials without question and he'd found them perfectly in order. Quite properly Konrad could tell him nothing of his present mission, but he had hinted that it had serious political implications and that his work might be gravely hampered by any meddling by irresponsible young amateurs.

"Did he really say that?" said Roger with interest.

"Perhaps not in exactly those words, but that's what it boiled down to. He certainly hinted that he had cause to complain of interference from outside."

"I see," said Roger.

"Now, touching on this affair," said Uncle Arnold, tapping his leg, "he was most co-operative. He agrees with me that it would be unwise to go to the police at this stage but he also agrees whole-heartedly that we should try to find out the truth —that's to say, who fired the shot, and whether in fact it was an accident or not."

"Were you able to sound him about Holtz?" I said.

"He doesn't like Holtz. I don't think he trusts him. But he was a bit cagey when it came to giving reasons. I wasn't surprised at that—in his job you've got to watch your tongue— and I was quite happy to leave it with him when he suggested he might make a few discreet inquiries. Even if he doesn't turn anything up we're no worse off."

Roger ummed non-committally and then said, "Did you find you had to tell him much, Uncle? You know, about our theories and so forth?"

"I said as little as possible, especially about Jimmy's activities." He looked at me severely. "But of course I had to give some reason for my suspicions. I did tell him the Holtzes were in the habit of going through our personal belongings and I explained this by suggesting they thought we were on to some illegal racket they were operating. Pretty flimsy, I know, but he seemed to accept it all right. He's a shrewd chap, you know."

"He must be," said Roger with a grin. "It's certainly thin evidence for suspecting somebody of shooting you."

"Maybe. But there you are. He may know more than he lets on. I did mention Hans, by the way."

"Oh?"

"Well, I pointed out that he left after a rather mysterious scene with Holtz and that it was something of a coincidence to get himself killed so soon afterwards."

"Did he have anything to say to that?"

"Yes, but it was an odd sort of answer. As far as I can remember his words he said, 'When the net is being tightened the big fish keeps his head. It's the small fry who blunder about in panic, and sometimes they can't even face the sight of the mesh.' Rather implying, you see, that Hans was up to his neck in it with the General and just couldn't face the music. But whether he was suggesting Hans was merely bolting, or that he deliberately chucked himself in front of a car I wouldn't know. He shut up like a clam after that. I think he felt he'd said too much already."

Roger and I went in to lunch soon afterwards. I was rather surprised to see both Grizelda and the General there, sitting at their old table. Grizelda half smiled and then quickly looked down at her plate. Her uncle gravely inclined his head.

We had barely sat down before Konrad came in. This time he didn't stop at the General's table but came straight over to us, the toothpaste smile much in evidence.

Neither of us asked him to join us but he managed it just the same, beginning by leaning over the back of a vacant chair and slithering into it as he talked.

As we had no doubt heard he had had a long chat with our uncle, the Major, and found him remarkably cheerful. A fine man, the Major, and it was a disgrace that this thing should have happened, a scandal, no less. He, Konrad, was sorry that our brief holiday was being spoiled by this regrettable incident, all the more so because as the instigator of the boar hunt he felt himself largely to blame. No, no, he insisted. He should have seen that better precautions were taken.

Perhaps he could make it up to us in some small way. He was driving into Hanover this afternoon, and as his business would take only about half an hour he would be delighted to act as our guide for the rest of the day. There were many interesting places to be seen, or we might care to go to the cinema. Afterwards, perhaps a little dinner somewhere, he knew just the place. . .

"It's awfully kind of you, Herr Konrad," said Roger, "but I'm afraid we've already made plans for to-day."

"Ah. You are driving yourselves into Hanover, perhaps. Or is it Braunsweig?"

"Well, no, as a matter of fact we're neither of us frightfully keen on towns. We thought of driving out a bit and doing some walking."

It was the first I'd heard of it, but I didn't say anything. Konrad nodded effusive agreement. "How right you are. There is nothing so stimulating as a long country walk. I wonder if you know . . ."

For the remainder of the meal Konrad aired his knowledge of the surrounding countryside, though it would have taken us several weeks to visit all the beauty spots he recommended. As we were leaving, Roger said casually, "By the way, Herr Konrad, I suppose you haven't a good map of the district? You know, something on a fairly big scale, with the footpaths marked."

Konrad shook his head regretfully. "I'm sorry, no. But Holtz is the man to see. Holtz will be sure to have one."

"Of course," said Roger. "Thanks for the suggestion."

Outside the door I said, "What's all this about long country walks? I thought you loathed them."

Roger grinned. "Just a little idea I had. Tell you later."

The first thing I looked for when we got to our room was Hans's album, and I breathed a sigh of relief to find it still in its place. Nevertheless, I knew from the way one or two things had been moved about that someone had been in the room, and when I pulled open my clothes drawers I felt pretty certain they'd been gone through too. Roger was equally sure about his.

"Holtz must be feeling absolutely livid," he said. "He'll just about throw a fit when he sees the mysterious newspaper parcel going out of the house again before he's had a chance to look inside."

"P'raps it would be better to wrap it in something else," I said.

"Good lord, why? I can't wait to see Holtz's face."

"Well, if we're going to hand it over to Grizelda, it's bound to centre the attention on her."

"See what you mean. Oh, well. I was going to ask Uncle Arnold if we could borrow the picnic hamper as well as the car. We'll shove it in there."

Roger went along to make his requests and came back in triumph bearing the hamper and Uncle Arnold's map. "All we have to do now," he said, "is lay in provisions. And my word, they'd better make a good job of it." He pressed the bell with a flourish.

We dumped the stuff in the Daimler and then went to look for Grizelda. We spotted her almost at once, walking in the rose gardens, and she quickened her steps to meet us.

"You have—made the arrangements?" she said softly.

It was Roger who answered. I saw from the beginning that he was determined to take charge.

"We can't really talk here," he said. "Look, Grizelda, do you think you could get away for an hour or two? We thought of going for a drive and a picnic. It'd be so much pleasanter—and safer—talking in the car."

She looked doubtful for a moment but then she said, "I must ask my uncle. It is possible that . . . Will you wait for me, please?"

She was gone only a few minutes and came back smiling radiantly. "It is all right," she said. "My uncle says it will be good for me to get away for a while. This is very nice."

Roger went on to get the car, and Grizelda and I walked more slowly after him. He was still studying the map when we joined him but he put it away with one of his secretive grins as I opened the door and we piled in the front with him.

At the entrance to the drive I fully expected him to turn down towards Kallendorf, but instead he swung left, following the track as it climbed parallel with the eastern margin of the Hochwald.

"We really *are* going into the country," I said.

"We certainly are. Still, this track is marked, even on Uncle Arnold's map. How well do you know this way, Grizelda?"

"I have walked for some distance by this road," she said. "I should warn you it becomes very bumpy."

"Not worse than this, surely," I said, as the big car bucked like a mustang and Roger wrestled with the wheel. "What about Uncle Arnold's springs?"

We went on for a couple of miles. Conversation was impossible. I began to wonder if Roger really knew what he was about.

Eventually we came to a cross-roads. I was reaching across for the map but Roger muttered, "This is it," and without hesitation turned left, still following the line of the forest.

"P'raps we should have brought a compass," I said.

"Have no fear," said Roger. "All is under control. We are now heading north-west."

A mile farther on he pulled off the road and brought the car to rest in a little glade in the fringe of trees. "There, my children," he said in a pleased sort of way, "no Holtz, no Konrad, no Willi. We can talk to our heart's content."

I said "No breath left either. You didn't really pick this spot off the map as the only suitable place for a chat?"

"Not altogether, no. But chat first. We've one or two things to tell you, Grizelda."

She listened attentively as we told her of our visit to the baker, Schmelling. Roger let me do most of the talking and her eyes never left my face as I repeated the conversations as faithfully as I could. She heard me to the end without an interruption, though a warm smile rewarded Schmelling's original plan to reserve for himself the "honour" of paying for Hans's funeral, and an involuntary "Oh!" escaped her as she realised the significance of the missing attaché-case.

Roger rounded it off. "So we now have something that Holtz would presumably give his eye-teeth for, and which may have cost poor old Hans his life. Though I must admit it's hard to see how you could blackmail someone with an extremely ancient snapshot album, from great-great-grandma onwards. However, it may mean more to you—Jimmy and I only had a quick squint at it. I'll get it for you."

While Roger was unlocking the boot Grizelda said with a puzzled frown, "And your uncle believes that Hans took his own life—threw himself in front of an automobile?"

"I didn't say so. That's Konrad's idea. Or rather, he dropped a hint. I shouldn't pay too much attention to it if I were you."

"I don't believe it," she said firmly. "Hans had nothing to be ashamed of. If it was not an accident then he was murdered."

Roger got back into the driving seat. "There it is," he said, and handed the album to Grizelda.

She looked at it in silence for a moment or two, then she said softly, "I have seen this book before. Hans used to let me look at it when I was a little girl in Berlin." She began slowly to turn the pages and we watched and waited for some sort of reaction.

They were all there, three or four generations of Grubers, and Grizelda seemed to know them all. Without referring to the neatly printed titles she was murmuring to herself, "*Grossvater und Grossmutter Gruber . . . Tante Mathilde . . . der Vetter Gustav . . . Onkel Karl Gruber . . .*" and giving little trills of laughter as she pointed to the Victorian dress, the moustaches, the studied poses. We turned over three generations. "Look, Hans as a baby. . . . Hans as a choirboy. . . . Hans as a young man—wasn't he good-looking?"

"Even if he looked like Elvis Presley," said Roger, "it still doesn't begin to make sense. It's nothing but a Gruber family portrait gallery. There's nothing here to give Holtz a hold over your uncle, Grizelda."

"You are right," said Grizelda slowly. "There is nothing here." She was staring at the last page in the album and I

couldn't fathom the expresssion in her eyes. "Perhaps it is
what is *not* here that is important."

At the top of the page were two pictures of Hans, looking
curiously ill at ease in uniform. In the centre of the blank
space below her finger was tracing the outline of where a third
photograph had once been. Traces of gum still clung here and
there to the coarse grey paper. Silently we waited for her to
go on.

There was a long pause and when at last she spoke again
her voice seemed to come to us out of the past.

"I remember this photograph so well. There were two men,
two soldiers, happy and smiling. One of them—the one who
stood here—was my father. Hans told me."

Roger glanced at me, wrinkling his brow, but I was as puzzled
as he was.

I said, "Do you mean that was the only photo of your father
you've ever seen? Surely your uncle must have some."

"No. After what Hans told me I asked my uncle for some
pictures of my father, but he said he had none. When I asked
him again another time he was quite angry and afterwards
never let me see the album again. Always he made some excuse
and quickly changed the subject. Of course, I was only about
eight years old, but I still remember how he looked in the
photograph. A strong face, he had, a little hard perhaps, in
spite of the smile. . ."

"I still don't understand," said Roger flatly. "Why should
you imagine a photograph of your father would provide Holtz
with a blackmail secret? There must have been something
else."

"I think there was something else," she said thoughtfully,
"but I can't remember . . . no, it's no use. I'm sorry." And
she smiled wistfully round at us.

Roger said, "Look, could you describe the photo? How they
were dressed and so on."

"How they were dressed?" She put her head in her hands
and thought deeply. "Yes, I think . . . the sort of clothes sportsmen wear. Like my uncle wore yesterday."

"But you said they were soldiers," Roger objected.

"Did I? Yes, well perhaps Hans told me. . . I can't remember, I suppose I must have had a reason for thinking . . ."

"Just a minute," I cut in. "The men—were they holding guns? Like we used yesterday?"

"Yes—yes, they were."

"And the other man—not your father—was he a rather fat man?"

She was looking at me in amazement. "Why, yes. I remember now, he was. But how . . ."

"Wearing a Tyrolean hat?"

"But Jimmy, how could you possibly know?" She looked from me to Roger and he grinned and nodded. "Uncle Arnold's story," he said. "Uncle Arnold's photograph, too, enlarged from this snapshot. Well, well." The grin faded as he suddenly realised the full significance of what we had just discovered.

"Please, Jimmy," Grizelda pleaded. "Tell me how you knew about the photograph, and what your uncle the major has to do with it."

We told her, as briefly as possible, wanting to spare her feelings. But it was impossible to gloss over the one outstanding fact—that her father had been a close associate and even an intimate friend of one of the major Nazi war criminals. She took it well, but I could see how badly shaken she was.

"Don't let it upset you, old girl," Roger said awkwardly. "After all, your father was a soldier with his duty to do. Don't suppose he was mixed up in any of the—well, you know, the beastly side of it. Camps and so on."

Roger can be a bit heavy-handed sometimes. She gave a little sob and hid her face.

The album had been resting in her lap and at that moment it began to slip off. Automatically I reached over to save it and as my fingers closed over the stiff cardboard cover I felt the little wedge of extra bulk under the paper facing on the inside. I pressed it gently with my thumb, and knew what it was without a shadow of doubt.

"Grizelda," I said softly, "I think I've found the snapshot."

Slowly she lifted her head and watched my finger as I drew it round the hidden oblong.

CHAPTER FOURTEEN

THE MAN TRAP

THERE WAS a long silence. Roger and I both seemed to feel that the next move was up to Grizelda, but she just sat there, staring at the blank outline of the only photograph of her father she had ever seen.

In the end she said, very softly, "I should dearly love to see his picture again, but I think I must take the album back as it is and ask my uncle to show it to me. There is still much here I don't understand. Perhaps now that I am older my uncle will explain."

"Well, I agree," said Roger. "It's a bit thick if you can blackmail someone just because his brother knew Hermann Goering."

"Not his brother," said Grizelda quietly. "Only his brother-in-law. My mother was sister to my uncle."

"I see. But it doesn't make any odds, does it. Quite a number of people must have known about it. I don't believe . . ."

"There's just one thing we may be forgetting," I interrupted. I turned to Grizelda. "Your uncle doesn't know Hans is dead and you don't want to tell him. You can't very well give him the album unless you do."

She looked pitifully forlorn. "But what am I to do? Please tell me what I can do."

I looked at Roger. I was dead keen to see the photograph and I guessed he was too, but it would have been terribly unfair to try and persuade her. "I don't know," I said.

Suddenly she made up her mind. "We shall open the cover," she said. "Has either of you a penknife?" The uncertainty had gone from her voice and there was even a hint of gaiety in her quick smile.

104

Roger fished a knife from his pocket and opened the small blade. "Shall I?" he murmured, and leaned over, slitting round the gummed edge of the paper facing. It came away quite easily and Grizelda turned it back like another page of the album. Underneath was a single, unfolded sheet of writing paper and on it, partially covering the bold, sprawling handwriting, lay the photograph.

It was almost exactly as I'd visualised it, except that the man on the right was rather younger than I'd expected. As Uncle Arnold had said, they both looked jolly pleased with themselves, particularly Goering. . .

"There can be no harm in our looking at the photograph, anyway," said Grizelda. "I've seen it several times before. Do you see what is written there?"

Along the lower margin, as with those of the Gruber family, Hans had printed in laborious capitals: "S.S. Obergruppen-feuhrer Erich von Kluge and Friend."

"I knew there was some reason why I thought they were soldiers," she said slowly. "But . . ." She shivered. "I was only tiny. Too young to realise what it really meant."

I felt a twinge of revulsion too. I'd read enough to know that the S.S.—the dreaded Blackshirts—had been guilty of every atrocity under the sun. One of their senior officers could scarcely have come out of it with clean hands.

Grizelda picked up the photo to look at it more closely. I hadn't meant to read it, but just then a word written on the paper underneath it seemed to shout aloud at me. From the start she gave I knew Grizelda had seen it too. It was her own name.

She hesitated only for a moment, then she said, "This letter concerns me. I believe I have the right to read it." She looked from Roger to me as if daring us to contradict her. I nodded and Roger said, "Jimmy and I'll take a stroll down the road. Just make sure there's nobody hanging about."

We gave her five minutes. When we got back to the car she was sitting just as we'd left her, the album still on her knee, staring into space. For a moment I was afraid she might be terribly upset by what she'd read, then she smiled the old, shy smile and said, "I feel so much happier now. I knew my uncle had done nothing dishonourable, and even my father . . . Listen, I shall read it to you."

I said, "Look, Grizelda, you don't have to, you know. If it's very personal . . . I mean, we shall still want to go on helping, even without knowing . . ."

She smiled again. "That's why you have a right to know. Listen." She picked up the letter and read:

> Quentella,
> Brazil
> 9th Sept., 1945

My Dear Brother-in-law,

Alas, the risks you took and the personal sacrifice you made to effect my escape to this godforsaken land have been in vain. Shortly after my arrival here I contracted a rare tropical disease and I now know that I have only a few more days to live.

With the end so near I am thankful for your one stipulation—that you should keep Grizelda and bring her up in ignorance of her father's shameful profession. I die happy knowing that she is happy and safe.

I am enclosing a certain photograph taken near the Hochwald shortly before the end of hostilities—you will perhaps recall that you granted me the favour of using the house for a week-end's sport. (What you must have thought of my neglect of duty!)

The truth is my friend of the photograph had acquired counterfeit foreign bonds and currency to the tune of several millions of marks and these, packed in waterproof boxes supposed to contain my personal effects, were concealed at Grauwasser.

For me, and for you I know, they may rot there, but for the sake of your reputation I beg that you will destroy them as soon as the opportunity arises. H.G. alone knows where they are hidden, but in case he has not survived I send you full instructions on the back of this photograph. Keep it safe until you are able to burn the accursed forgeries.

My strength is failing. Embrace Grizelda for me.
With eternal gratitude,
Erich v. K.

I think we had scarcely breathed as we listened to Grizelda's soft voice speaking the tragic words. For some moments after she had finished there was dead silence in the car.

"Well," muttered Roger at length. "So that's what they're after. Obviously they never got hold of the photograph, or they'd have found the stuff ages ago. What does it say on the back, Grizelda?"

She turned it over. " 'Second chamber. Eight metres east of red stone. Shelf concealed by overhang.' "

"Golly," breathed Roger. He looked at me eagerly. "The pond—lake—whatever it was, on Holtz's map. . . I suppose you didn't happen to notice what . . ."

"Yes," I said. "It's called the Grauwasser." I turned to Grizelda. "Did you know there was a tiny lake somewhere in the middle of the Hochwald?" She shook her head in wonderment. "Well, there is, and that's where the boxes are still hidden. If Goering hadn't committed suicide rather than face trial . . . but as your father anticipated, H.G. did not survive."

Even as I said it a startling thought struck me. "Just a minute," I said excitedly. "Could I read the letter again, Grizelda?"

I read it through twice, and then I knew for certain. "H.G. See? Same error, like the hat. It wasn't Goering who helped hide the stuff, it was Hans. That was why Hans mustn't be known to have lived here before. The penny might have dropped with Holtz, like it did with me. Then . . ."

"Don't go so fast," said Roger peevishly. "I still don't see what . . ."

"Look," I said. "They got hold of the letter and black-mailed the General for helping . . ." I decided not to say "a war criminal" and made a quick substitution. ". . . Grizelda's father to escape. Holtz made himself hotel manager as a cover and started hunting for the loot but without the photo it was bound to be a long job and the photo was stuck in Hans's album where he had no reason to look for it. But once he knew who Hans really was he'd have been on to him like a ton of bricks."

"Hang it, I can see all that," Roger protested. "What I don't see is why Hans was brought here in the first place. Wouldn't it have been safer to keep him and his album well out of the way?"

"Well . . ." I was beginning doubtfully, when Grizelda said, "I think I can explain. I believe my uncle would never have permitted Holtz to succeed. There is a chance he may never find the boxes if they are well hidden. But if he were lucky— then my uncle would go to the authorities in spite of the disgrace that Holtz would bring upon him. Hans was merely to report progress. He was a spy, if you like."

"Mm," said Roger uncertainly. "You may be right, of course. . ."

"I'm sure I am right," she said. "On the back of the letter are a few lines written by Hans. Listen. 'Forgive my disobedience but they are very close and I was desperate. Thank God I was successful in finding the letter. Thank God, mein General, your honour is safe. I hope I may be spared to see them denounced.' "

Once again I had a feeling almost of reverence. "What a wonderful chap he was," I said.

"He was," Roger agreed soberly. "If Holtz should get away with this . . ."

"Which he stands a fair chance of doing. 'They are very close' was what Hans said."

"Yes, well it's high time someone else took a hand, and that, Jimmy old son, means you and me." Roger picked up Uncle Arnold's map and stared at it intently for some moments before he went on, "We thought the key to the thing was hidden in the Hochwald. Now we know it is. When I brought us here I had a vague notion of getting in by the back door and doing some exploring round this Grauwasser place. But now that we know what to look for and where to look for it—well, we'd be missing the chance of a lifetime if we didn't go. Holtz thinks we're safely off on a nice country jaunt and anyway he never leaves the house in the daytime. . ."

I reached over for the map. "All very well and good," I said, "if we had a decent map. This one doesn't even show the lake."

Roger grinned in a self-satisfied way. "I may not have your gift for languages, old man, but I flatter myself I can read a map. I happened to notice from Holtz's that most of the main tracks through the forest radiate from the Grauwasser area, and although this one's only a small-scale affair there are still a few tracks marked. See? I reckon we're sitting just opposite *that* one."

I looked at the untrodden pathway through the trees and then back at the map, where Roger had stabbed an almost indistinguishable hairline with the point of his penknife.

"How on earth can you be sure," I said.

"Well, I can't be positive, but they all lead roughly in the right direction. I should say it's about a mile to a mile and a half—say half an hour's walk. Forty minutes at the outside. What do you say?"

"Fair enough," I said, "but what about Grizelda?" and "What about the car?" said Grizelda at the same moment. We looked at each other and laughed.

"The car's easy," said Roger. "We'll run her a few yards into the trees. Nobody'll see her from the road. But Grizelda —well . . ." He grinned at her. "If she'd like to wait in the car it would be safer, of course. . ."

She seemed on the point of stamping her foot. "I should not like to wait in the car. If Hans could do what he did for my uncle surely I, whom he has loved as a daughter, can take one or two tiny risks for him."

"Somehow," said Roger, "I had a feeling you'd say something like that. Now then, young Jimmy, we might just do a bit of a check on this track. . ."

I said, "I knew we should have brought that compass."

He ignored me and went and stood looking up at the tallest tree. "Quite simple. Toss you for who goes up."

I won, and I went up. It wasn't a difficult tree to climb, but thirty feet or so from the ground the trunk had thinned considerably and there was quite a bit of movement in the wind. At forty feet I had the impression of being in the crow's nest of a light schooner riding an Atlantic gale. I looked down at the ground once and decided not to do it again. Hanging on grimly with one hand and shading my eyes from the sun with the other I peered out to the south-west.

There was still a veiling of foliage where some trees rose above their neighbours, but I could see well enough to distinguish an area of higher ground where some trees seemed to be of a different colour. I thought I could even make out a few pinnacles of jutting rock interspersed with the greenery. The track below me appeared to lead exactly in the right direction.

"It's all right," I said when I rejoined the others. "You can't see the track for very far, but it certainly starts off all right."

"There will be other tracks crossing this one," said Grizelda. "We must be careful not to stray on to one of these."

I said, "A compass would have been a help, certainly."

"Bah!" said Roger. "All you need is a sense of direction."

But he underestimated either the distance or the hazards of pathfinding, or both. Forty minutes later Grizelda and I were waiting on the now poorly defined track while Roger climbed his second tree. I had climbed my second ten minutes earlier.

"You're not worrying, are you?" I said. "We may have missed the track, but we can't really go wrong as long as there are trees to climb. The only snag will be going back—we can hardly expect to come out exactly by the car."

"I'm not worrying," she smiled. "This is fun. You would never believe how dull life at 'der Grun Specht' was before you came."

Roger jumped down the last eight or nine feet of his tree. "You're right there," he said. "Jimmy certainly hotted things up, didn't he? Well, my children . . ." He faced about and pointed almost at right angles to the track. "That's where we want to be—about two hundred yards over there. I'm afraid

it'll mean blazing a trail through the undergrowth.   Okay?
Then follow me."

We followed dutifully.

Actually it was less than two hundred yards before the whole
character of the forest began to change. The ground began to
slope upwards, the tall pines became sparser and gave way to
overgrown Christmas trees which in their turn dwindled into
dwarf shrubs and bushes. Here and there an outcrop of grey
stone thrust itself through the springy turf. We started to
climb in earnest.

Five minutes later Roger called back, "There's the track
again—see? We may as well get back on to it." He struck off
at a tangent and Grizelda and I followed a curving spur of
higher ground to meet up with him.

The track swung a little in our direction, so that we
approached it almost simultaneously. "We'll try not to lose
it going back," Roger was saying, when Grizelda gave a little
scream. "Stop!"

We froze in our tracks and looked at her in amazement.
"What's up?" said Roger.

"Look!"   And she pointed at the ground a yard in front of
Roger.

Actually it was the stake she'd seen first—had in fact stubbed
her toe against—imbedded in the ground with a length of steel
cable running from it. The trap itself was half buried on the
track, almost invisible under a sprinkling of soil and bits of
turf. Roger bent forward and peered at it intently. "Golly,"
he breathed. "What a wicked-looking object."

We were all a bit shaken. "Surely this sort of thing isn't
legal in Germany, even on private land," I said.

Grizelda shook her head emphatically. "Even on private
land it is forbidden, and this is not private land. Sometimes
the peasants use such traps for catching the boar, but I don't
think this one was laid for such a purpose."

"I don't think it was either," said Roger. "It's got the Holtz
trade-mark all over it. Can either of you see a nice hefty
stick."

We found a strong length of dead wood and he gingerly poked

away the camouflage until the trigger was exposed. "All right," said Roger. "Stand clear." And he gave it a hearty whack.

The thing reared up as if it was alive and the jaws snapped together viciously. Roger looked at Grizelda and his face was very serious. "Thanks," he said. "I always was one for putting my foot in it. I nearly did it once too often." He looked down again at the trap. "Perhaps we won't stick to the path after all."

We went on cautiously, searching the ground. I said, "There were seven or eight tracks leading to this part. Do you reckon they've set traps on all of them?"

"I expect so," said Roger coolly. "I should think Willi's been having a lovely time. Just wait till I get hold of him, that's all."

I grinned to myself. It had been a near go and Roger wasn't going to forget about it in a hurry. Willi was for it, all right.

We were in the open now. The ground was strewn with grey boulders, and massive slabs of rock dwarfed the few stunted trees that clung to the unfriendly soil. It was an odd phenomenon, this queer little bald patch in the middle of the forest.

A dozen yards to our right the track squeezed through a gully formed by two big shelves of rock. We clambered over to find that we had reached our objective. The pool lay before us.

CHAPTER FIFTEEN

THE SILENT WATCHER

WE LOOKED into a rocky bowl whose sides sheered down to the still, dark waters forty feet below. Moss and wild rock plants spattered the grey, unfriendly stone and here and there a stunted bush clung to its foothold in a little crack or crevice. Nearer the water a few thin, straggling trees and clumps of yellowing rushes eked out a sunless existence.

It was an eerie place, gloomy and forbidding, and I think we were all a little overawed as we stood there in silence. Roger was the first to speak.

"You see what it is," he said in a low voice. "Or what it was, rather. A stony quarry. Accounts for the number of tracks leading here. Probably a thriving industry a hundred years ago. The Green Woodpecker was built of this stuff for a start."

We went closer and peered over the edge. Immediately below us a narrow ledge jutted away from the rock face and extended for twenty feet or so just above the surface of the water. On the extreme right of it a couple of sturdy planks bridged the twelve-foot gap to the last foothold of a path that wound precariously around a full quarter circle of the pit. On the left a big tarpaulin sheet weighted at the corners with heavy stones evidently concealed something of considerable bulk.

"Well, there's only one way down," said Roger. "Looks at bit tricky. Think you can manage it, Grizelda?"

She scorned to reply and we walked round the quarry, following the imprints of heavy boots superimposed over and over again by Holtz and Willi during many nights of vain searching.

Standing above the faint beginnings of the pathway we could now see the cave above the ledge, a yawning mouth extending the length of the ledge and almost as high.

"Man-made, you can tell," said Roger authoritatively.

"They were after the best stone, you see. Had to follow the vein wherever it went. This ought to be a piece of cake."

"You did bring the photograph, I suppose," I said.

"Of course."

"You don't think perhaps—we should have brought the album as well," suggested Grizelda hesitantly. "Just to be quite safe."

"Lord, no. It's safe enough locked in the boot and this looks like a two-hand job. Not to worry, Grizelda."

We began to scramble down the path. It wasn't difficult at first because there were plenty of handholds, but Roger led the way and put Grizelda in the middle in case of any tricky bits. Nearer the ledge the going was more difficult; tufts of grass came away under our hands and down by the water the rocks were covered in a treacherous green slime. Here and there they'd been deeply scored by nailed boots which were really the only sensible footwear. Grizelda's light heeled shoes in particular were highly unsuitable for this sort of thing and after a while she stooped down and took them off, turning to me with a smile and saying, "Have you a pocket?"

We arrived at the bridge. The planks only just reached across and strong as they were and however carefully we walked they still bounced a good deal. In the middle it was rather like being on a trampoline, and when my turn came to cross I had a nasty feeling that the end behind me was slipping. The water below looked horribly cold.

We went straight over and lifted the tarpaulin. It was quite a collection we saw. The mine detector—confirmed as such by Roger the moment he set eyes upon it—was there, also a diving suit and helmet, air-line, air-pump, flashlamps and a varied assortment of excavating tools.

"I was right about the helmet," said Roger with satisfaction. "I suppose they started off by searching the pool." He laughed aloud. "Just think of the happy hours Willi must have spent waddling about among the weeds and the tadpoles."

The cave faced north and not a ray of watery sunlight was reflected from the surface of the pool. We peered vainly into the gloom.

"There isn't time to hang about," said Roger, taking charge again. "Come on, grab a flashlamp apiece."

Fortunately there were four to choose from. We picked the three brightest and went into the cave. It was like walking into a refrigerator.

The cave floor began by sloping slightly upwards but after thirty or forty paces it suddenly changed direction and began to shelve gently down again. The roof, which had begun by being well clear of our heads, was a good deal lower now and I could just touch it if I reached up on tiptoe.

"Anyone suffer from claustrophobia?" said Roger in a low voice that nevertheless raised hollow echoes all around us. "If it goes on like this we shall be crawling soon."

I said, "If it goes on like this we're more likely to be swimming. We must be about at the level of the pool outside."

The air seemed to be getting even colder. Like a tomb, I thought, and found myself shivering at the idea. In the combined light from three torches the cave walls gleamed wetly, streaked with colour ranging from brilliant orange to a dull purple. Infrequently at first, but growing larger and more numerous, black puddles hung about the floor and water dripping from the roof kept up an insistent "plop-plop-plop."

"Second chamber," Roger muttered. "I don't get it. Are we in the first, would you say?"

"I doubt it," I said. "It's just been a sort of passage so far, narrower than when it started if anything. I think we shall find . . . oh lord, look."

We'd come about a hundred and fifty yards; the cave walls were less than fifteen feet apart and my hair was wet through from brushing against the roof. Roger and Grizelda swung their torches in line with mine and we stopped dead, gazing in dismay. Beyond the limit of the probing beams the cold, black water seemed to stretch interminably into the darkness.

We went closer. "This is the first chamber all right," said Roger. "It's getting wider already. And the roof's higher. Shine your torches round this side."

By the water's edge the cave walls suddenly swung out in a huge arc and were still widening beyond the range of our flashlamps. The roof was reaching up and up and looked curiously vaulted, like a cathedral. Or a tomb.

"Nothing doing this side," Roger reported. "Try the other. There must be some way round it—there must be."

Obediently we switched our lights to the right. It looked a lot more promising. Hugging the wall, a sort of shelf about two feet wide rose just clear of the water, and as far as we could see continued indefinitely.

"Tricky," said Roger, "but not impossible, to begin with, anyway. I don't know about Grizelda, though. . ." He looked at her doubtfully. "It'd be a bit lonely, I know, but it might be better if you waited for us here. Shouldn't take us long to . . ."

"Oh, please, no," she said pleadingly. "I'm good at climbing, really I am."

"Yes, but even so . . . it slopes nastily here and there, see?" He flashed his torch along the shelf again. "And it looks as slippery as the devil."

"Please."

He looked at her quizzically for a moment, then shrugged and turned to step forward on to the narrow shelf. "Right," he said. "This way for the pirates' hoard."

Grizelda looked round to smile shyly at me. "Stay close behind," she whispered, "to catch me if I slip."

I said, "I'll try. Give me your shoes again. Better cold feet than a cold bath."

I bent down and dipped my fingers in the water. "Golly, cold's right. It's got no right to be still liquid. It ought to be a solid block of ice."

Actually the going was easier than it had at first looked. The walls hereabouts were pitted with holes and crevices that offered ample handholds and as we went on these frequently deepened into wide recesses so that from time to time we could even walk two abreast.

"What we're looking for is some sort of passage through to this second chamber," said Roger over his shoulder. "If we miss it we're likely to finish up where we started from."

"We won't do that," I pointed out, "because this ledge

doesn't go all the way round. Probably only as far as the passage."

"Yes, well we can't be sure, so keep your eyes open."

We went on more slowly, flashing our torches into all the deeper clefts. Once Roger called "Eureka!" and Grizelda and I hurried forward to join him in the mouth of a tunnel very much like the one that led to the first chamber, but after a dozen yards we came up against a blank wall.

"The stuff petered out, you see," said Roger knowingly. "Never mind, next time lucky."

As we walked back towards the black water Grizelda whispered to me, "I know it's silly, but I can't help feeling that we are being watched."

It was so exactly what I was feeling myself that I very nearly blurted out an admission, but I stopped myself in time and was able to say casually, "Very natural. It's the eeriness of the place, of course. Enough to give anyone the creeps. Except Roger, perhaps," I added as an afterthought.

"He's wonderful, isn't he," she said enthusiastically.

"It's just that he hasn't any imagination," I said, and was surprised to hear how peevish my voice sounded.

Roger was quite a bit ahead again and suddenly his voice drifted back, charged with incredible heartiness, "Walk up, walk up. This way for the pleasure boats. Round the bay for five bob, ladies and gents. Walk up."

"What the dickens . . . ?"

Our shelf had broadened considerably; from the towering wall to where it dipped gently into the water was about nine or ten feet. As we came up to where Roger was standing we could see that he was examining a very old, very disreputable rowing dinghy that had been drawn up out of the water on to this natural landing stage.

"You can't get any farther," said Roger. "Look." He swung the beam of his torch. A few yards ahead the shelf ended abruptly and the still water reached and clung to the sheer wall of the cavern.

"Just as well," Roger went on, "that Holtz has got as far as this in his search or we'd have been stuck ourselves." He set his flashlamp down on the centre seat of the dinghy. "Well, come on, Jimmy, we can't waste time. Give me a hand getting her into the water."

"I suppose it floats," I said doubtfully.

"Oh yes, my friend," said a voice behind us. "It floats remarkably well."

We spun round to see Holtz standing there, a heavy automatic pistol in his hand.

CHAPTER SIXTEEN

THE SECOND CHAMBER

MY HEART was going like a sledge-hammer. From her quick breathing beside me I knew Grizelda was feeling much as I was. Holtz came a little closer, but not too close. He wasn't taking any chances of any of us going for the gun. Speaking for myself I'd no intention of trying.

"My apologies for startling you," he said ironically. "I have been waiting for some time—in the little cave behind me." He made a slight gesture with his head but his eyes remained fixed on us and the hand holding the gun never wavered. "I felt sure you would not be able to resist coming after you saw the map. And the letter. And—something else, perhaps?"

He snapped on the pocket torch he held in his left hand. "Turn out your flashlamps," he ordered. Grizelda and I obediently switched off ours. Roger was leaning over to reach the one he'd put down in the dinghy when Holtz snapped, "Leave that one turned on. I like it there."

There was dead silence for a moment. Then Roger cleared his throat and said, without a quaver in his voice, "Look here, Holtz, I don't know what you think you're playing at, but I warn you . . ."

"Shut your mouth!" Holtz almost screamed the words. "*You* are warning *me*? Fools of English boys, interfering in matters that are not of your concern. It is *I* who am warning *you* that if you do not do exactly as I direct you . . ." His voice fell again to its familiar level of smooth civility. "You will please to turn out your pockets and place the contents on the ground before you. You first," he said, directing the beam of his torch at me.

I emptied my pockets; two or three letters, fountain pen, three handkerchiefs (I can't imagine why), a couple of pencil stubs, a length of string, a box of matches and an extraordinary variety of small odds and ends. Holtz examined the little pile warily, without ever relaxing his watch upon our slightest move. Then he bent down and picked up the box of matches. "You may replace your belongings," he said. "You next, Fraulein. Have you a handbag?"

"No."

The steady beam moved searchingly over her. "No pockets, either?"

"No."

"Very well. Your turn, my friend," he said to Roger.

Roger seemed to have accumulated more junk even than I had. The pile grew higher as he emptied pocket after pocket. "Is that all?" Holtz said at length.

"Yes."

Holtz smiled disbelievingly. "I wonder."

I wasn't the only one to notice that Roger hadn't touched the top pocket of his jacket. Holtz's first and second fingers reached in and came out holding the precious snapshot.

If we expected him to give any signs of wild delight we were disappointed. He turned it over in his fingers, glanced briefly at the writing on the reverse, and then to my utter amazement replaced it in Roger's pocket.

He prodded the pile of odds and ends with his foot. "And the letter?" he demanded.

Roger was silent. Holtz glowered at him for a moment or two, then turned his attention to Grizelda and me. "The letter?" he said again.

Here it comes, I thought. He's going to threaten to shoot if we don't tell him. I wanted to shout aloud, "It's in the car, with the album!" but something, some obstinate little demon at the back of my mind, held my tongue. Grizelda's hand brushed against mine, seeking comfort. It was trembling violently. I took it and squeezed it hard, to hide the trembling of my own.

Holtz nodded thoughtfully. "Never mind," he said. "I shall find it. In the automobile, no doubt. With a—a certain package?"

It was put as a question but I doubt if he expected an answer, nor I think, did he need one. One look at our faces must have been enough. He smiled with his lips and nodded again.

"You may take up your property," he said to Roger, and when he had done so, "All of you, place your flashlamps in the bows of the boat. We are taking a little trip."

I suppose we must have gaped a good bit. "But why not," he said, the smile touching his lips again. "You are anxious, are you not, to see this hiding-place? So you," pointing the gun at me, "in the stern. Perhaps you will assist Fraulein von Kluge to take her place beside you. That is well. . . . Now," he motioned Roger forward, "we push together, and you . . . will row."

The dinghy slid into the water, rocking crazily as first Roger, then Holtz clambered over the side. The light from Holtz's torch threw grotesque weaving shadows on the dimly-seen wall behind us and the little boat settled low in the water as Holtz took his place in the bows.

"Row," he said again, and as Roger picked up the oars, "We are already in deep water. Keep to the side."

We began to move slowly forward, the oars creaking like old bones. I had the impression that Holtz had put the gun down on the seat beside him and from the occasional "clank" of metal I concluded he was doing something with the flashlamps at his feet, but his attention never wavered for an instant as he continued to give Roger his directions. We crept along, hugging the wall.

After a while Holtz said conversationally, "It may be some surprise to you to learn that this pool has a diameter of two hundred and sixty metres. Amazing, is it not? The temperature of the water remains constant at six degrees centigrade. That is very cold indeed. Willi, like the fool he is, fell in one night. He was in the water for two or three minutes only, but was half dead with the cold before I could get him out. You can all swim?"

Nobody answered. Holtz prodded Roger in the back. "You. You can swim?"

"Yes," said Roger.

"And your brother?"

"Yes."

"And you, Fraulein?"

"No," she whispered.

"Then we must be careful not to capsize the boat as we alight. The landing arrangements are not at all convenient. It was there that Willi fell in."

After this cheery announcement we went on in silence for a bit. What's he up to? I kept on asking myself. What on earth is he up to? Is he going to make us carry the stuff out for him? If so, what then? He can't afford to let us go, not after this. And over and over again the phrase went on echoing in my head, "He can't let us go, he can't let us go . . ."

"What is he going to do?" Grizelda whispered.

"I don't know. What time did you say you'd be back?"

"I said probably between five and six."

I looked at my watch. It was only half past four.

We seemed to have been rowing for hours when Holtz said sharply, "Draw in to the side. Not too fast . . . gently, gently. . . ." He leaned over the side and eased the shock as the bows ground against the rough stone. Then immediately he stood up and climbed on to a ledge some three feet above us, taking with him a coil of the mooring rope which he looped round a handy pinnacle of rock.

"You may each bring a flashlamp," he said, "b not be used without my permission. You unders well, you first." And he directed the beam of his torch at Roger.

One by one we joined him on the ledge. I badly wanted a chance to talk to Roger, but Holtz gave us no opportunity, moving us on with a wave of his torch and keeping only a couple of paces behind us.

It was the passage through to the second chamber all right, but not in the least what I'd expected. The ground rose in what appeared to be gigantic rough-hewn steps, or terraces, narrowing as we went up until we seemed to be walking through a tunnel. Then suddenly we were going down again, down into the second chamber. . .

Holtz's torch threw a strong beam, but it was scarcely enough to give a well-defined picture of the scene. I merely had a vague impression of a sprawling network of stone banks, separated by black, yawning chasms, as if the whole place had been rent by some freakish earth tremor.

"Halt!" ordered Holtz. Willingly we obeyed; there was no means of telling where we went from there.

"From this point," said Holtz, "our progress will be slow and precarious. One false step means death—you will soon see why. This cavern was much undermined and there have been many falls of rock, even recently. We shall therefore walk singly and you, Fraulein, will lead us. Do not fear. I shall be close behind to direct you. . ."

"Look here," burst out Roger. "Can't she wait here for us? If she promises not to move, I mean?"

"No, my friend. That would not do at all. I must have some security."

"Well, let one of us go in front, then."

"No." He rapped it out like a sergeant-major. "Let us proceed. Fraulein. . ."

"I suppose at least we can switch our lamps on," Roger said.

"No. It will not be necessary. Come, Fraulein."

Holtz had said our progress would be slow and precarious and he hadn't understated it. He seemed to know where he was going all right, but for the life of me I couldn't tell how. It was a maze of crumbling stone ramparts arching and rearing and twisting above great gulfs of darkness. Once Holtz stopped and shone his torch into the void. Faintly answering was the glint of water twenty or thirty feet below.

"You see?" said Holtz pleasantly. "No hope of rescue. Do not slip or—make a false move."

Once I thought I'd gone. The loose stuff under my feet feet shifted suddenly and I lurched forward, dropping on all fours as the only means of recovering my balance. When I got up my legs were trembling like jelly and my heart pounding in my throat.

"All right, old man?" said Roger.

I managed a hoarse, "Yes, thanks," though my mouth was like blotting paper.

"Look here, Holtz," Roger said, "my brother very nearly went over just then. He can't see a thing at the back there. We must use the other lamps. It's just plain silly."

After a moment's hesitation Holtz said, "Very well, turn on your lamp."

With relief I fumbled for the switch of mine. Nothing happened. I turned it the other way. Still no light. From the muttering in front of me Roger was apparently having the same experience. "It won't come on," he said at length. "What have you done to it?"

"Mine won't, either," I said softly.

There was silence for a moment, then Holtz said briskly, "It was necessary to put the lamps out of commission. Proceed, Fraulein."

"What's he up to?" I whispered to Roger. "Any idea at all?"

"Not a clue. Hang on, old man. We might get a chance to jump him later. If we could only get hold of his torch . . ."

"No talking in the ranks," barked Holtz. He seemed to be thoroughly enjoying himself.

We went on, inch by inch, step by step. Sometimes the causeway underfoot was six or seven feet wide, sometimes as little as three. There was one ghastly stretch when I'll swear it was less than eighteen inches, and the surface was loose into the bargain. We stumbled along, crouching low for the sake of balance, not daring to look right or left; blindly following the moving blob of light as Holtz unerringly picked his way above twin valleys of death.

Suddenly he stopped dead, so that Roger and I very nearly blundered into him. The beam of light lifted to illuminate a great bastion of stone ahead and slightly to our right. In the surrounding darkness it seemed to glow with a rich crimson radiance of its own.

"The red stone," Holtz said softly. He went on, speaking to Grizelda, "So much trouble might have been avoided if your father had only been more explicit in his letter. So many nights of fruitless searching . . . and all the time that doddering old fool of a waiter held the secret. . ."

"So you killed him!" Grizelda whispered in a voice trembling with horror.

"Of course. Gruber was a danger to me. He had to die."

"And we?" she breathed. "Are we not a danger?"

He laughed strangely. "No. From you I have nothing to fear. Come, Fraulein. We change direction here. To your left, please."

I counted eight paces, as nearly as I could from our shuffling progress, and Holtz stopped again.

"We have arrived, my friends," he announced in a loud voice. "X marks the spot, and the spot is *there*." He dipped the torch suddenly and we saw below us a ramshackle platform constructed of lengths of rough timber. Below again, far below, the glint of still water.

"So you . . . found it," I said, breaking the taut silence.

"Last night, finally. The mine detector confirmed my suspicions—the Obergruppenfeuhrer had obligingly scratched an arrow on the red stone. But I was three hours, with Willi's doubtful assistance, bringing up the wood for the platform. There have been falls, you see, since 1945," he explained, and went on cryptically, "There may be more. To-night, perhaps."

He picked up a stone and tossed it carelessly over the edge. I counted five before the faint answering "plop" drifted up to our straining ears.

Holtz said, "You will climb down to my platform, all of you. I should like you to see for yourselves this cunning hiding-place that has cost you," he hesitated, ". . . so much foolish effort."

Something in his voice, a sort of controlled exultation, sent cold shivers up my spine. Dimly I began to see . . .

Roger was seeing it too. "I don't think we'll bother, Holtz," he said. "Quite prepared to take your word for it that you've got what you were looking for. Very clever of you to think of using a mine detector, too. Without it I suppose you might have . . ."

As he rattled on he was edging closer and closer to Holtz,

and I knew he was going to make a desperate attempt to grab the gun. I held my breath.

"Do not come any closer, my friend," Holtz said calmly. "I am holding Fraulein von Kluge's arm. It would be most unfortunate if she lost her balance. . . . Now then. You will show the way. Then your brother. Fraulein, you last."

There was no alternative. Roger lowered himself over the edge and climbed down with comparative ease, using foot and handholds cut into the stone perhaps by Holtz, perhaps by Grizelda's father sixteen years before. I followed, then Grizelda. We stood huddled together on that cramped little platform with a thirty-foot drop on every side except one. And there, at the mouth of a deep cleft, in gloom only half relieved by the failing beam from Holtz's torch, were three tin trunks, lids thrown back, quite empty.

CHAPTER SEVENTEEN

THE VALLEYS OF DEATH

"THE LIGHT is not good?" came Holtz's voice. Almost concerned, he sounded. "Wait. I shall fit a fresh battery."

Darkness came down like a blanket. Grizelda gripped my arm and I could feel her trembling violently. Nobody spoke. There was something paralysing about the blackness.

Then the beam shot out again and played on us steadily as we clung there, not daring to move. Holtz laughed shortly. "Speaking of batteries," he said, "I must now confess that I have substituted those in your flashlamps for used ones. Frankly, I do not think you will ever be found—an overturned boat in the first cavern should be explanation enough if the good General thinks to search Grauwasser—but if you are foolish enough to attempt to find your way back in the dark, a venture, I must warn you, that can only end in disaster, then the reason for that disaster will be plain for anyone to see. I am leaving you now, my friends. Farewell!"

The beam swung up and darkness came again. We listened in tense silence as the faint shuffling and the occasional fall of loose stones passed overhead and died away.

Grizelda was crying softly. "Well," I said roughly to Roger, "what are we going to do?"

"Get off this confounded platform, to start with," he said. "There isn't room to breathe here. Hang on to my coat, Grizelda. We're going into the cleft. Don't worry, I've got a mental picture of it."

It was a relief to be doing anything at all. We edged forward inch by inch until suddenly I heard a clank as Roger knocked against one of the tin boxes. A few moments later we were each sitting on one of them.

"That's better," said Roger. "Now. Start thinking. We've got to have a light of some sort. Holtz was quite right. We'd never find our way through that maze in the dark, and even if we tried one of us would be bound to take a false step sooner or later. Jimmy, Holtz took your box of matches. Are you sure you haven't got an odd one tucked away somewhere? I haven't. I've already looked.

I went carefully through every pocket and then went through them again. There wasn't even a dead matchstick, let alone a live one.

"There's just one thing we might try," Roger said. "These batteries. They're dud, I know, but the three joined in series might give us a bit of light from one bulb. Thank goodness Holtz left me my little coil of wire. You take the batteries out, Jimmy, while I cut this into lengths."

It was a tricky business in the dark, but I managed it in the end. Then we had to wait five minutes or so while Roger did his connecting up.

"I'll strap them together with the rest of the wire," he said, half to himself, "but the connections won't be very wonderful. Just have to keep our fingers crossed."

He must have made the last connection as he said it, because a dim glow suddenly illuminated the cleft and our waiting, anxious faces.

"It's not very bright, is it?" he said, and broke the connection again. "Can't afford to waste it. Now, we've got to think. What's the time, Jimmy?"

"Twenty to six," I said. I was surprised to find it wasn't later.

"Twenty to six. And Holtz has been gone about ten minutes. Any idea how long it took us to come from where we left the boat?"

"I looked at my watch on the boat. About forty minutes, I suppose."

"Mm. He'll probably be quicker going back. Look, I'm going up there to keep tabs on him. That torch of his should be visible for miles. You two stay here. As soon as his light disappears I'll come down and we'll make a start."

"Will it—will our light last out?" I said.

"It can't last very long. I'm more worried about its being

bright enough." There was a sort of resigned hopelessness in his voice that I hadn't heard before. I felt my scalp prickle as he groped his way past me. "Aren't you going to put it on now?" I said.

"I can manage." The platform creaked as he stepped on to it and we sat and listened to the faint scuffling and scraping as he began to climb.

From time to time I called, "All right?" and each time he replied with a breathless "Yes." Five minutes went by. "All right?" I called.

"All right. Just—about there."

"He's nearly there," I said to Grizelda. "It's going to be all right, you'll see."

"I'm not frightened now," she said. "Only terribly, terribly sorry that I've brought you and Roger to this. Forgive me, please."

"There's nothing to forgive," I said. "This time to-morrow we'll be laughing about it."

"I shall never laugh about it. Never."

Roger's voice came to us, cloaked with echoes. "I'm at the top. Can see his light all right and he's well on the way. Shouldn't be long now."

But it was fully twenty minutes before he finally called, "All clear. I'm coming down."

"Can't we just come up?" I said.

"No. The first part's very tricky in the dark. I just had a bit of luck, that's all. Better if I come down."

Anxiously we waited. The scuffling got gradually nearer and we kept on talking to him to keep him going in the right direction. Suddenly he gave an exclamation and a shower of small stones poured down, some bouncing on the platform before they went on into the void below.

"All right, Roger?" I couldn't keep the fear out of my voice.

"I think so. It's just that . . ." Suddenly the scuffling again, and more stones, then the dreaded half scream and the thud as his body hit the platform. . .

"Hang on," I cried chokingly and blindly groped my way

forward. I found him at once. At first I thought he was hanging on by his hands, then I realised that he'd miraculously found another foothold below the platform. The light planks groaned and shook as he pushed and I heaved, but in a matter of moments he was beside me. We knelt there, getting our breath back. Then Roger said, "It's tricky, that bit. Gosh, it's tricky. And I don't see how I can manage the light *and* climb. Well, we'll just have to go terribly carefully, that's all. Test every step. . ."

"Roger," I said, "there's one more possibility. When you fell—you must have steel tips on your shoes—the sparks were like a firework display. If we only had something dry enough to use as tinder, we could cut spills from the planks here, enough to light us all the way."

"Flint and steel," he said softly. "You're right, Jimmy. A lot of this rock must be flint. But tinder. . . What did they use in the old tinder boxes?"

"Quite a number of things, I think. It just had to be quite dry."

"Yes, but it's got to be inflammable too. Paper?"

"I don't think so," I said. "Very thin shavings, or something like that would do, but . . ."

"But we haven't got any. I know. What else *have* we got? Go through your pockets again."

Grizelda's voice came out of the darkness. "There is something you will both have in your pockets. All men have. That is fluff."

"Fluff! Gosh, she's right. Go through your pockets, Jimmy, and collect every bit. And don't lose any."

Back in the cleft we pried into every corner of every pocket and then slit our jacket linings with Roger's penknife, putting each precious pinch of fluff into an envelope which Grizelda held. Eventually the envelope was half full.

"That ought to be ample," Roger said. "Turn the top down, Grizelda, and hang on to it. Now, what we want is a nice chunk of flint."

He rigged up the lamp again and by its feeble light we searched the rocks about us, scratching with the penknife to produce the best display of sparks. The most satisfactory stone we found lying on the platform where it had landed during Roger's fall.

We hacked slices off one of the planks and then cut them down into long slivers until we had about a hundred. These we split into three bundles and tied them together with my string. Then at Roger's insistence we cut a whole lot more...

"Aren't we being frightfully optimistic?" I said. "I mean, all these preparations, and it may not work at all."

Roger said, "It's got to work. Make some paper spills from those letters of yours. Now then, Grizelda, where's that envelope?"

The sparks flew as Roger drew the blade of his knife over the flint and we waited, not daring to breathe. Twice the fluff glowed faintly red and we blew gently into the envelope, but it refused to ignite. After three or four minutes of it Roger said, "There's just one more chance. Warm it."

"In our hands, you mean?"

"No. Too damp. Pack it round the bulb and run the batteries."

"But—we'd be using up all the light we have . . ."

Roger said soberly, "Quite honestly, old man, we're taking a gamble either way. And I think this is the best chance."

I didn't argue. We packed the stuff against the reflector, leaving a tiny hole in the middle, and then sat and waited...
The pitiful yellow glow slowly turned to an insipid orange as ten minutes went by.

"It'll have to do," Roger said. "We'll leave it where it is. Ready with your bit of paper, Jimmy?"

It was as well that I was. As the sparks fell in a bright cluster the fluff began to glow redly and at our first gentle puff it burst into flame. I thrust in my spill and it kindled a split second before the leaping flames died.

"Good work," breathed Roger. "Get another one going, quick!"

We got three paper spills alight and then started on the wooden ones. With three of these safely burning I felt like sobbing with relief. Grizelda was laughing excitedly with the tears streaming down her face.

We'd arranged the spare spills and a little heap of odd chippings under the platform so that we could set it on fire to give us plenty of light for the climb up to the top. That was Roger's idea. Also we'd tied one end of my ball of string to the plank farthest from this point so that when it was alight we could haul it up to give us a man-sized torch. I thought of that one and as I was going last I was carrying the other end of the string.

We thrust a spill into the kindling and it blazed up at once. Within seconds one side of the platform was well alight and for the first time for an hour and a half we could see what we were doing. There was rather more smoke than we'd bargained for but it didn't bother us too much. And the platform continued to burn, that was the main thing. Steadily, testing every hold, we went up.

Suddenly Roger gave an exclamation. His spill had gone out. A few moments later I brushed mine against the rock and it, too, died in a shower of sparks. I looked up anxiously at Grizelda. She was calmly lighting a fresh spill from the stub of her old one.

Roger scrambled over the top and helped Grizelda the last few feet. By the time I joined them the light from our fire was failing. As far as we could tell only the last plank was still burning. With infinite care we began to haul on the string.

The plank came up well at first; it wasn't very heavy and the string was pretty strong, but there was one thing we'd overlooked. Hanging down as it was, with the flames growing stronger and reaching higher, it was only a question of time before the string caught fire. We hauled faster but the string was already smouldering.

"Keep going," I muttered, and threw myself flat on the ground, reaching over as far as I dared. The blazing plank was directly underneath, smoke was swirling up and choking me. With my eyes streaming I groped down and felt the unburned end come into my hand. As my fingers closed on it I suddenly felt its weight. The string had snapped.

I don't know how I got it up. Desperation must have given
my fingers extraordinary strength. But a few seconds later
Roger was saying, "Nice work, old man. Nice work. I didn't
like to mention it before but I think we may have under-
estimated how many spills we should want. Now we can just
keep one going for emergencies. Well, come on. No point in
hanging about."

As we moved off after him Grizelda squeezed my arm.
"Well done, Jimmy," she said softly.

The burning plank gave us a better light than Holtz's torch
had done, and by seeing a greater area we were able to keep
our direction more easily than I'd expected. But it was half-
burned away when we started and at the end of fifteen minutes
Roger said, "I think we'll have to save the rest of this for spills.
All light up, chaps."

It was reassuring to see how much light we still got, and a
wonderful relief, too, to find that we all had a remarkable
recollection of the route. As we plodded on my thoughts began
to run on beyond the immediate urgency of finding our way
safely out of the second chamber. Until then it had been a
question of first things first. Now the problem of getting
through the first chamber began to loom. In the end I put it
to Roger.

"Only one thing to do," he said coolly. "One of us will have
to swim. Get hold of the boat if possible, if not, fetch help.
How far did Holtz say it was?"

"Two hundred and sixty metres."

"I'll go. Do it on my head."

"Oh, no," Grizelda protested. "Remember what he said
about the cold. You couldn't, you couldn't."

Roger said, "Haven't you heard about the people who bathe
on Christmas Day?"

A few moments later we saw flickering shadows on the
towering wall above the passage and stepped thankfully on to
more solid ground.

"How many spills have we got?" said Roger.

I had six, Grizelda five, and he two.

"Come on, then. No time to waste."

As we marched through the passage I said, "That's going to be the snag."

"What is?"

"Light. How are you going to see where you're going? You might be swimming round in circles."

"I'll keep to the side, then."

"It'll make it much longer."

"Well, it can't be helped, can it?" said Roger irritably.

We came down to the water. It didn't look any warmer than it had before.

"Well, here goes," said Roger, and began peeling off his coat.

"Wait," said Grizelda suddenly. "There must be another way. When my father came—he would not have a boat. How did he and Hans manage?"

"Well, that's true. But look, you can see there isn't another way now. Perhaps a fall . . ."

Inspiration suddenly dawned on me. "The water level," I said excitedly. "Wouldn't it rise according to the level of the Grauwasser? It was June when they hid the stuff, remember. Now it's March and there's been a lot of rain lately."

Roger said, "We can soon find out." He went to the end of our little jetty and lay flat, reaching down with a long spill.

"Well, well," he said. He stood up and we peered at the stick in the uncertain light. Only four inches of it were wet.

"It's a shelf," Roger said. "What's the betting it runs all the way, just below the surface?"

CHAPTER EIGHTEEN

KONRAD LENDS A HELPING HAND

THE SHELF seemed to be about five feet wide. We lowered ourselves into the water and it came just over our ankles. Roger led the way, as usual, sliding his feet along the smooth stone in case of any sudden drop. After two or three minutes of it my feet were becoming painful with the cold and I began to wonder how we should stick it out.

"How's it going, Grizelda?" Roger called back. "Think you'll be able to bear it?"

"It is—very cold," she gasped. "But I think my feet are getting numb. That will perhaps be better."

"I'd give anything for a pair of gum-boots," I said. The searing cold was sheer agony now.

We went on in silence for about a hundred yards, then the shelf began to dip until the water reached our knees. Another few steps and it was deeper still.

"Go on a bit farther," Roger said between his teeth. "It must come up again, surely."

"If it doesn't we've had it," I said, though I could hardly speak, my teeth were chattering so. "Grizelda can't swim, remember."

"Ah!" Roger stopped suddenly, then we saw him step up in the water. It was uncanny.

"Good-oh!" he called. "We're back again to four inches."

Apart from one more shorter dip we went for the rest of the way with the water sloshing just above our ankles. Then suddenly we were out of it. The relief in our aching feet was indescribable.

"Look," I said, and pointed. At the limit of the area lighted by our spills we could just distinguish the dim outline of the boat, floating upside down on the water.

"Didn't forget a thing, did he?" said Roger. "Well, let's

hope he overlooked that pile of stuff outside. There ought still to be an odd flashlamp there and I'm relying on it to get us home. It's going to be pitch dark outside."

It was, and it was raining too. Anxiously we searched the ledge at the mouth of the cave but every item of equipment was gone.

"Chucked it in the lake, I suppose," Roger said. "Well, what are we going to do? Try and make it in the dark—and don't forget the booby traps—or camp here till morning?"

"Wait," I said, gripping his arm. "Listen."

Through the gentle swishing of the rain came the sound of a motor-car engine in low gear.

"Oh, no!" said Roger. "Not again. Look, Jimmy, you get that side of the cave and I'll stay here with Grizelda. We'll jump him as he comes in. All right?"

We took up our positions and waited. The engine sounded close now, a high-pitched note that suddenly came down to a growl and then cut out altogether. Men's voices, we heard, coming nearer.

"It's—it's Uncle Arnold," I said, hardly daring to believe it myself. I ran out on to the ledge, shouting, "Uncle! Uncle Arnold! We're here!"

The voices murmured confusedly above, then a strong beam of light swept down and focused on the ledge.

"It's them!" I heard Uncle Arnold say. "Thank heavens, it's them." His voice bellowed over the quarry, "All right, we're coming. How the devil do we get down?"

We shouted instructions. Lights flickered and weaved about, then two began to move down the winding path towards us. One remained; on account of his leg and much against his will, Uncle Arnold had been persuaded to remain aloft. Throughout his companions' descent his anxious questions to us were interspersed with impatient exhortations to them to hurry.

At last two dim figures crossed the rickety bridge. I'd had an uncomfortable feeling all along that Holtz might have destroyed that too, but of course it would have been out of keeping with his careful plans to suggest an accident.

An American voice spoke out of the darkness. "Hallo there, boys and girls. Guess you could do with some light down here."

He introduced himself. "Johnny Vermont. And this," he swung his torch to illuminate the stolid features of a man in the uniform of the German police, "well, I guess I don't know his name but he's a darned good driver. Gee, folks, when I decided to come this evening instead of to-morrow all I figured on was a nice cosy chat about old times with the Major. And what do I find? A situation that makes most paperback thrillers look like bedtime stories for the tots and your uncle half crazed with worry. Not that I blamed him. When they found Holtz dead that way and Willi blew his top . . ."

"What!" we exclaimed in unison.

"Yes—well, I guess we'd better let the Major do the explaining. If we don't get back up there soon he'll be coming down looking for us."

Uncle Arnold wouldn't say or listen to a word until he'd got us all packed in the vehicle, which I recognised at once as Holtz's Volkswagen. The wooden-faced policeman got in the driving seat and we moved off slowly down the muddy, rutted track.

"Now," said Uncle Arnold. "Tell me. Everything."

We told him, though with everyone making excited contributions it must have been more than a little confusing. However, after a few final questions he seemed satisfied he'd at last got the story straight.

"Now then," we said. "What about Holtz?"

"Yes. Well, Holtz is dead—shot. Suicide, apparently."

"But why? He'd got the stuff—probably stacked away in the garage." I glanced at the policeman but he hadn't understood a word. "He was as pleased as Punch when we last saw him. Why go and shoot himself?"

Uncle Arnold wriggled his leg into a more comfortable position, grunting to himself. "It's odd," he said, "the way things turn out. It was soon after you three left this afternoon that a police car rolled up at the hotel and a couple of German bobbies were asking for Holtz. He couldn't be found. They said they were making inquiries about a case of hit-and-run driving in the village. Of course I didn't know about your interview with the baker but I did realise the victim must be Hans. Eventually they asked to see the car—this car—and Willi had to open up the garage for them. He didn't want to one little bit, I could see that. They poked around for a bit and then said they'd be back later."

He paused. "Well, go on, Uncle," said Roger impatiently. "You can't stop there."

"No. Well, to tell you the truth, I'll have to let Johnny carry on from there. You see, just after six that confounded doctor arrived and—well, turned a bit awkward. Made me get back into bed and so forth."

"You'd been up all afternoon!" I said accusingly.

"Eh? Well, not really. Just pottering about, you know. Anyway," he hurried on, "Johnny arrived about then and walked right into it. Tell them, Johnny."

Johnny said, "Well, it was this way. I hustled through my work and decided to slip down this afternoon instead of to-morrow. Just this side of Hanover a police car shot ahead of me. I didn't think anything of it at the time but when I reached the hotel there it was in the yard. There was a guy in uniform at the door and an *unter-offizier* interviewing people in the lobby. They made me sit down and said they might have to ask me some questions. It seemed they'd come looking for Holtz again and this time they found him. Only he was dead—lying shot through the head in the garage."

"Sounds as if he was planning to do a bunk," said Roger, "and left it too late. Still, I must say I'm surprised he took that way out."

"What time did you say this was?" I asked Johnny.

"About half after six. Maybe a little later."

It certainly seemed to tie up. Holtz couldn't have been back long.

"But what did Willi say?" Grizelda asked anxiously.

"Willi. Yes, he certainly started something. They'd had a go at Frau Holtz but she didn't help them any. Then they hauled

Willi out of the cellar—he was hiding there scared out of his wits. Gibbering like a crazy kid, he was, about money and caves and so on—it sounded like something out of the Arabian Nights. I guess nobody was taking him seriously till he accused the General."

"He said my uncle had—had killed Holtz?"

"He did, Fraulein. And then all this rigmarole about Nazi loot planted under the bench in the garage—he said the General would stop at nothing to prevent his father having it."

"And I suppose they found it there," I said.

"Found it nothing. They went through that garage with a toothcomb, but no dice. Willi's stock was lower than zero, but he wasn't through yet. The final thing was this spiel about you three being marooned up there by the Grauwasser. The cops thought it was a great story and began laughing themselves sick, but I could see your uncle and the General didn't think it so funny."

"It was turned seven, you see," said Uncle Arnold by way of explanation. "I was getting worried about you in any case. Then somehow—I don't know, it sounded fantastic, but this yarn of Willi's had the ring of truth. I could see the General thought so too. I got Johnny to tell this sergeant fellow we must go and make sure, and in the end he agreed on the condition that one of his men came with us. But he wouldn't let the General come even though the old boy seemed to inspire an incredible amount of respect."

"Is my uncle—arrested, then?" said Grizelda.

"I don't believe so," Uncle Arnold said gently. "But I understand they may be taking him into Hanover. Apparently he's agreed to make a statement of some kind to the Chief of Police."

Grizelda didn't answer. I leaned towards her and said softly, "It shouldn't be necessary now, should it?"

It was half past eight when we got back to the house. There were two cars with engines running standing in the courtyard —the police car and Konrad's Mercedes.

Konrad came bouncing across and greeted us effusively. He

was so very relieved to see us safe and sound. Had Holtz really done all that Willi claimed he had done? Had he, really? But it was monstrous, monstrous. No wonder he had killed himself —with this dreadful thing on his conscience. . .

"You don't believe, then, that my uncle shot him?" said Grizelda.

"But, Fraulein, it is inconceivable. Excuse me, please, I hear the sergeant calling me."

He was away only a few seconds and caught us up before we went indoors.

"Fraulein, your uncle the General is in the police car. They are taking him to Hanover to make a statement. The sergeant asks that you will please accompany them. And he requests a few words with you too, Major."

"Of course," said Uncle Arnold, and hobbled off.

Grizelda took my hand and squeezed it gently. "We shall be back to-morrow, I'm sure," she said.

"If you're not," I said, "we'll come and get you."

Konrad stood looking at her retreating back. "There goes a young lady of great courage," he said reflectively. "A pity that . . ." He turned back to Roger and me and went on briskly, "I regret that I must be going too. They require also a statement from me."

"Which way are you going?" Roger asked him.

"To Hanover. The route is immaterial. If I can be of any assistance . . ."

"It's the car," Roger explained. "Our car. Don't like to leave her up there by the forest all night. If you could possibly give me a lift . . ."

"I shall be delighted."

"Thanks awfully. Just give me a couple of minutes to get into a dry pair of trousers."

I had a quick bath and felt a lot better. The ordeal of a few hours back already seemed to belong to the dim past. While I was dressing Uncle Arnold and Johnny came in.

"Well, that's that," said Uncle Arnold. "I hope, anyway. We've got to trot into Hanover some time to-morrow to sign statements but we can make a day of it and do the town. Where's Roger?"

He was none too pleased when I told him. "He'd no right to go off again like that," said Uncle Arnold peevishly. "Haven't I had worries enough for one day?"

I said, "He should be back any moment," but he merely grunted and looked fierce.

Johnny was looking preoccupied. After prowling around the room for some time without speaking, he suddenly turned towards us and said flatly, "I'm still not satisfied."

Uncle Arnold stopped looking fierce and his eyebrows shot up. "Well, you take some pleasing, that's all I can say. What more do you want? An earthquake?"

Johnny sat down on the bed and began to fiddle with his pince-nez, polishing them furiously with a handkerchief.

"It's just—well, just a bit too tidy, I guess. The big bad wolf is dead so we can wrap the case up and file it away. But— I wonder. From what you told me, Major, on the drive up to the Grauwasser, I'd say there's still a whole lot of questions still to be answered."

"Such as?" demanded Uncle Arnold.

"Such as why Holtz ever let you come here in the first place. How he got to know of the hidden loot in the first place. And," Johnny paused significantly, "what's happened to it."

Somewhere at the back of my mind I felt the answer to all his questions was buried under the welter of impressions and events of the past few days. I tried to concentrate, but it wouldn't come.

Johnny went on, "When I first wrote Holtz to make your reservations I had a letter back to say they weren't taking any bookings for the next few weeks. I was pretty sore about it and I decided to drive down on the chance I could make Holtz see sense. There was a guy came to see me from N.A.T.O. that morning and I happened to mention to him that hotels that didn't function as hotels should be exposed. Then, oddly enough, a couple of days later came a letter saying there'd been a mistake and the reservations were okay."

"Who was the man you spoke to?" asked Uncle Arnold.

"He was the same guy who came to see me some time last summer. Some trivial difficulty about oil supplies. But on that occasion he happened to notice Hermann's hat. A war memento," he explained for my benefit, "that I keep on my desk. Asked a lot of questions about it and seemed very interested. N.A.T.O.," Johnny said thoughtfully. "He'd have access to a lot of secret stuff. If it was believed Goering did stash away a little nest egg this gave him a pretty clear indication of where to start looking."

"But who was it?" said Uncle Arnold irritably. "His name, man."

"You didn't guess? It was . . ."

"Konrad," I said. Suddenly all the remaining bits of the jig-saw clicked into place. That was why the General's house in Berlin was searched. That was why fake evidence had to be manufactured to disgrace him. That was why Hans was suddenly desperate to recover the letter—because Konrad had recognised him as the General's servant. That was why Kurt lied—no doubt Konrad knew something of his past too. Konrad was the blackmailer-in-chief. Konrad was at the back of everything. . . .

Suddenly my heart stopped beating and my throat went dry. I looked at my watch.

"Roger's been gone three-quarters of an hour," I said hoarsely, "and we left the letter in the car."

CHAPTER NINETEEN

THE DOG THAT BARKED

THEY STARED at me uncomprehending. "We couldn't tell you everything," I said desperately, "because it wasn't our secret. But it's a letter that Holtz—Konrad—both of them, I suppose, were blackmailing the General with. If Konrad could get it back he'd feel safe again. And don't you see—Roger . . ."

Johnny whistled softly. "Does Konrad know it's there?"

"Holtz knew. If Konrad spoke to him after he got back. . ."

Johnny smacked the palm of his hand with his fist. "You can bet your sweet life he did. And shot him. That's why they never found the stuff—it was already stacked in Konrad's Mercedes."

"Come on, Johnny," Uncle Arnold rapped out from the doorway. "Never mind that now." His face was set and there were beads of perspiration on his forehead. "Where exactly did you say the car was?"

"Along the road by the forest. About three miles. Not more than four anyway. They've had time to go there and back twice."

"What are we waiting for, then?" said Johnny. "My car's round the front. Let's go."

Kurt was just coming along the corridor as we went out. He began to speak and then trailed off with the word "dinner" on his lips as we shouldered past him without paying the slightest attention. Johnny's car was parked right outside the door, an enormous black Cadillac. We piled in and he started with a jerk that threw us back against the cushions. It was pitch dark and pouring with rain.

"Turn left at the end of the drive," I said. "But you won't be able to go very fast. It's an awful road."

Johnny paid little heed to my warning. He was in a hurry and he just put his foot down and kept it there. We might as well have been on the Hamburg-Berlin autobahn.

The Cadillac lurched and swayed, fighting the rutted surface. As I peered ahead, where the headlamps slashed a dazzling path through the driving rain, I thought, if Roger is coming back and we meet him now it'll be all up. There wasn't room to pass a bicycle.

But Roger wasn't coming back, and when at last we slid to a halt on the muddy grass at the side of the track we found only the Daimler, half hidden in the trees where Roger had left her. Of Roger himself and of Konrad there was no sign.

Uncle Arnold wasted no time in useless tut-tutting. "Got a torch, Johnny?"

"Sure. Right here."

Johnny reached into a pocket on the dashboard and handed out a big torch. Uncle Arnold immediately began studying the ground, walking about and muttering to himself. "Ah. There's the Daimler's tread, nearly washed out. I'd know that anywhere. Now then, unless he pulled off before we did . . ." He stopped suddenly. "Johnny! Jimmy! Come here!"

We ran over. "Careful where you go. Come behind me. Now then. See that?" He pointed to a pair of tyre marks, sharp, and fresh in the soft mud. "That's where he pulled off. Now the point is, did he turn round?" We followed the twin treads, slightly shallower now, as they led in a gentle sweep to the road.

"If he was going to turn, this is where he'd do it. There's nowhere else he could. So he went on. With Roger, the swine. Now, why did he go on? Where's it lead to?"

"I've a map," Johnny said. "Good one. We'll find out."

We got back into the Cadillac. Johnny put on the interior light and spread his map out over the steering wheel.

"See here, there are two possible routes back to the Hanover road," he said. "They may be no more than cart-tracks, but then so's this. After the second turning the road just fizzles out. He had to take one of those two."

"Go on," said Uncle Arnold. "We don't know how much start he's had but we've got to find him. We'll stop at the first police station we come to on the Hanover road."

We tore through the darkness, Uncle Arnold reading from

the map on his knee. It was about a mile and a half to the first turning. We slithered to a stop in the middle of the road and peered out desperately through the car windows.

"Listen," said Uncle Arnold suddenly. "Turn off the engine."

Above the pattering of the rain we heard a dog barking somewhere close at hand.

"Where there's a dog there are usually people," said Uncle Arnold. We got out and stood in the slush, trying to fix the direction.

"Isn't that a light?" I said. "Just there, behind the trees?"

"Good boy. Come on." Uncle Arnold stumped off at a speed that would have amazed Doktor Stein and Johnny and I followed.

It was a tiny farmhouse in a terrible state of disrepair. Uncle Arnold hammered on the door and the dog at the back worked himself up into a frenzy. We had to knock twice more before the door was finally opened on a chain by a little man with a face the colour and texture of a dried-up orange.

"*Guten abend, mein Herr*," said Johnny, and went on in German, "I wonder if by chance you have seen or heard a car pass this way within the last half an hour? We seem to have missed some friends of ours."

The old man put a hand up to his ear. "*Bitte?*" he croaked. Oh, lord, I thought, this is going to be hopeless.

"Have you seen another car?" shouted Johnny.

"No, I ain't. Don't see so well as I used to. I ain't seen nothing."

"What's he saying?" demanded Uncle Arnold.

"Saying he can't help us. Anyone else in the house?" bawled Johnny.

"Nary a soul. Only my old bitch Inge, an' I put her out in the back when she set up that barking. Can't abide it when she goes on like that."

"How long ago?" said Johnny quickly.

"'Bout ten minutes since. When yon car went by."

"But you said . . . oh, never mind." Johnny turned to Uncle Arnold. "The dog was barking about ten minutes ago, at a

car, he thinks. But that doesn't help us any. It might have
gone either way." He pulled a couple of notes out of his
pocket and the old man's eyes nearly popped out of his wizened
little head as he reached for the money with a claw-like hand.

We were walking back to the road when the door-chain
rattled again and the old man called, "Her'll have gone that
way." His skinny arm was pointing along the road we were on.

"How do you know?" shouted Johnny.

"Only barks like that, my old bitch, when they goes past the
house, not when they goes t'other road."

We ran back to the car. "He may be talking through his
hat," said Johnny, "but it's the only chance we've got."

The road made no pretence now at being anything more
than a cart-track, two muddy parallel lines with grass sprouting
between them. Johnny's knuckles gleamed white in the dim
torchlight as he fought to keep the car on a level course, but
he never slackened speed.

"Coming up to the second turning now," Uncle Arnold was
saying, when Johnny rapped out, "Look!"

"Where?" said Uncle Arnold. "Confound this rain."

"Car lights," I breathed.

Three hundred yards ahead, twin red glow-worms winked
through the slashing rain.

"He's stopped," said Johnny in surprise, and Uncle Arnold
muttered, "Pray God we're in time."

Our blazing headlamps rent the darkness as the mighty
Cadillac bucked and roared like an enraged monster bearing
down on its prey. Now we could see the black outline of the
Mercedes—and something else besides. Two figures were
fighting desperately—wrestling, swaying drunkenly from one
side of the road to the other.

"Pull in behind," ordered Uncle Arnold, his hand on the
door handle. As Johnny braked and the Cadillac lurched and
slithered to a stop we saw Konrad make a tremendous effort and
throw Roger heavily towards the far ditch. Then he was
running for the Mercedes.

Johnny and I had half covered the distance when we heard
the door slam and the engine roar into life. We closed on the

car, he from one side, I from the other. I was actually touching the rear door handle when the wheels spun, gripped, and the car leaped forward. Konrad swung the wheel hard over and against all the odds on that soft ground the Mercedes responded, coming round to the right in a tight arc that brought him within inches of the ditch. Then he was on firmer ground and accelerating, heading for the Hanover road.

Panting, Johnny and I turned to find Uncle Arnold holding Roger by the arm and firing anxious questions at him. Roger looked a bit shaken but he managed to grin at us as we came up.

"Second close shave to-day," he said. "Never mind, you can get used to it."

"Well, you won't get the opportunity of having a third," Uncle Arnold said firmly. "From now on I'm not letting either of you out of my sight. What your parents would say if they knew the half of what . . ."

"Fair enough," said Roger. "We'll stick together from now on. But look, shouldn't we be getting on? He's got quite a start already."

I thought Uncle Arnold would throw a fit. He spluttered and snorted and finally burst out, "If you think there's going to be any more fun and games to-night, Roger my boy, you're jolly well mistaken. You may enjoy playing cops and robbers, but the responsibility's too much for me. From now on the authorities can do their own dirty work."

"But—but he's got the letter." Roger looked at me. "You guessed that was what he was after, of course."

I said, "Yes, but Uncle still doesn't know much about that side of it. So it isn't so easy for him to see . . ."

"I've seen quite enough, thank you," said Uncle Arnold grimly. "Turn her round, Johnny."

"But Uncle," Roger persisted, as Johnny started the motor, "just think. We went through all that business this afternoon so that the police needn't be brought in . . ."

"Well, now they have been. You could hardly expect them to stay out where violent death is concerned. And they very nearly had another to investigate—yours."

"But the old General—he's done nothing dishonourable,

has he, Jimmy? It'll finish him if all this has to come out."

"The General has gone to Hanover of his own free will to make a statement—in all probability has made it already. It's too late, Roger."

"It may not be," I said eagerly. "Grizelda went too. She'll have told him the letter's safe."

"Stop!" thundered Uncle Arnold. "Stop badgering me from all sides. Is it conceivable that I should agree to a mad chase all over Germany after a desperate armed man?"

"But he isn't, Uncle. Not now. I got rid of the gun."

Johnny stopped in the middle of turning the car round and Uncle Arnold said, "Did you now? I wondered when we could skip all this flummery about letters and get on to what happened. Well?"

"He's got a dickens of a start," Roger said plaintively. "Couldn't you take my word for it now and let me tell you about it later?"

"No, Roger."

"Well, there isn't really much. He didn't show his hand till we got to where I'd left the Daimler. Then, while I was thanking him and getting out the keys he suddenly hauled out this gun and said he wanted the letter. He said if I didn't get it for him he'd have to shoot me and get it himself. So I unlocked the boot."

"Reasonable," I said.

"Quiet, Jimmy," said Uncle Arnold.

Roger went on, "He took the album with the letter in it and marched me in front of him to the Merc. Made me get in, got in himself, put the gun in his pocket and drove on. I reckoned I was being taken for a ride, as they say, and I don't mind telling you I had the wind up properly."

"Never mind," I murmured. "So did we."

"We went on and on until we seemed to be in the middle of nowhere. Eventually he stopped the car, got out the gun again and just sat there, smoking a cigarette and telling me how clever he was. I was beginning to think things were looking up when he chucked away the cigarette and told me to get out. That," said Roger, with what I couldn't help feeling was a masterly example of understatement, "was rather a nasty moment.

"Well, anyway I got out and stood there bracing myself for a last desperate attempt to rush him. Then the miracle happened and your lights suddenly flashed over the brow of a hill. His attention wandered for a split second and I grabbed the muzzle of his gun, twisting it at the same time. I got it away and chucked it over my head. I think it fell somewhere—somewhere over there," said Roger vaguely.

I looked round. Konrad had certainly picked his spot. It must have been about the loneliest place in all Germany.

There was silence but for the incessant beating of the rain. "Well, Uncle?" said Roger. "There it is. We're three to one, and he's unarmed. What do you say now? He's got a bit of a start but you could catch him up, couldn't you, Johnny?"

"Oh, sure," said Johnny laconically. He looked at Uncle Arnold. "Well, the decision's yours, Major."

CHAPTER TWENTY

UP IN SMOKE

UNCLE ARNOLD tapped the map on his knee. "Look at it," he said. "Just look at those roads. He might have taken any one of them. We shouldn't have a dog's chance of finding him."

I said, "He was supposed to be making for Hanover. Anyway, he's got an office there. Ten to one he'll make for Hanover."

Uncle Arnold looked round at us and smiled wryly. "It's all very well for you young bloods, and for you too, Johnny Vermont, but I've got a fearful responsibility. If my brother had any idea of the dangers you've been exposed to and the sort of larks you're proposing now . . ."

"May as well be hung for a sheep as a lamb," murmured Roger.

Uncle Arnold burst out laughing. "You young rascal!" He looked down at the map. "Why, it's all of twenty-five miles to Hanover."

"Half an hour's run," said Johnny, edging the car into gear.

"Dinner waiting for us . . ."

"Give us time to work up an appetite," said Johnny, taking off the brake.

"Now, wait a moment, I haven't given my permission yet . . ."

"No, but you will," said Johnny, and let in the clutch. The Cadillac leaped forward and he swung the wheel hard to the right.

We drove for four or five minutes in silence. I had the impression that Uncle Arnold was still fighting a mental battle, his sense of responsibility pitted against a desire we all shared to get even with Konrad. I wondered which was winning.

"Village coming up," said Johnny.

Uncle Arnold automatically referred to the map. "Karls-dorf," he said absently. Then he turned and rapped out, "You are sure he's unarmed, Roger?"

"Absolutely," said Roger.

"All right. We'll go on for a bit. But listen, all of you. No violence. Understand? I'm not going to have us all land up in a German jail. Straight on, Johnny."

We roared through the village, its single dark, deserted street echoing the hiss of our tyres.

"Two more villages," said Uncle Arnold, "then we hit the Hanover road about five miles north of Kallendorf."

It had stopped raining, but the muddy little road was completely waterlogged. Every now and again our wheels threw up a spout of water that reached to the tops of the car windows. We couldn't maintain a very good speed but we had the consolation that Konrad couldn't be doing any better.

It was a relief to get on to the road that three days before had brought us from Hanover to the lonely hotel in the shadow of the Hochwald. Briefly the moon came out and the cobbles gleamed silver.

The huge Cadillac bore down on Kallendorf; although it was only half past nine there were few lights in the houses and the main street was silent and deserted.

Two miles farther on we saw the tail lights of a car ahead. We were gaining on it rapidly. Roger and I were thumping on the back of the front seat, and even Uncle Arnold couldn't contain himself. "Come on, old girl," he was saying, as he gently tapped the dashboard.

It took us half a mile to overhaul the car in front. As we flashed by, our faces crowding the near-side windows, we burst out laughing as a startled little man peeked up at us from the driving seat of a tiny Opel.

The villages came and went; Kreideberg, Heinzdorf, Lingen, Eisendorf. . . . As we thundered through Eisendorf I happened by the merest chance to glance down a side street leading off the village square. There was a man in a telephone box at the corner of the street and the Mercedes was parked a dozen yards down.

"There he is," I yelled.

Johnny braked hard and threw the car in reverse. But Konrad had seen us. As we came back to the widening of the square the Mercedes's headlamps blazed and we heard the roar of her exhaust.

"Block him, man, block him," bawled Uncle Arnold. Johnny went into forward gear again and swung the wheel over hard. The Cadillac lay broadside across the road, completely blocking it as we wrenched at the door handles and streamed out.

But Konrad didn't hesitate. The Mercedes shot out of the side road and turned right, heading back the way we'd come.

We lost several precious seconds turning round and by the time we were clear of Eisendorf there was no sign of the Mercedes. We strained our eyes for the tell-tale glow of her tail lights as the speedometer needle mounted . . .

"Got to pick him up soon," muttered Uncle Arnold, "or he'll give us the slip . . . ah! Did you see?"

"Sure did," said Johnny. "'Bout half a mile ahead. We'll catch him."

At Heinzdorf we were about five hundred yards behind and by the time we reached Kreideberg we'd reduced Konrad's lead to half that. But we couldn't gain another inch. Konrad was driving like a madman.

The sparse lights of Kallendorf came into view. "What'll he do now?" said Roger. "Surely not make for The Green Woodpecker."

"Look at *that*!" There was exultation in Johnny's voice. "Now we've got him."

By the size and height of the lights it was a heavy lorry lumbering out of Kallendorf. It didn't seem possible for Konrad to pass it. He fell back and we picked up a hundred yards, but that was all. Perhaps he saw us coming up in the driving mirror and panicked, perhaps he tried to reach a slightly wider stretch of road, we never knew. With a fresh surge of speed he raced on, while the monster ahead held the very middle of the road.

It was all over in a few seconds. Konrad swerved at the last moment, his near-side wheels mounting the over-grown, rutted verge. For a moment we thought he'd done it, but at the last moment he must have hit a bump. The Mercedes reared up like a living thing, crashed down on two wheels, held it for an impossibly long second and fell quietly on her side.

We ran up and found Konrad lying limp and oddly contorted with his head almost touching the long grass that reached up through the broken window on the passenger's side. Somehow we got his door open—it was like opening the lid of an enormous box. While the lorry driver sat in his cab mouthing rich German oaths we managed to pull Konrad clear. We carried him back twenty yards to the lights of the Cadillac, and as we laid him down a sheet of flame enveloped the wrecked Mercedes. Within seconds it was a blazing inferno.

Konrad stirred and raised his head a little. Then he spoke, though we had to bend down to catch the words. "Tell the General not to worry. All his troubles are going up . . . in smoke." Then a little smile, a travesty of the flashing toothpaste smile of old, passed over his face and his head fell back.

"I think he's dead," said Uncle Arnold soberly.

There was suddenly the hum of another car, coming fast from the direction of Hanover.

"Stop him, Roger," said Uncle Arnold. "We don't want another tragedy."

Roger stepped out into the road, but the car was already slowing down. "It's the police," he called back to us.

The police car pulled up and we waited as two men in uniform got out and walked up to us.

"It's the sergeant," said Johnny in surprise. "*Guten abend*, Sergeant Müller. I'm afraid there's been an accident."

"Ah, Herr Vermont. And the English major, I see. *Guten abend, Herr Major.*" He saluted stiffly and then got down by Konrad's body, staying there for some moments without speaking. When he finally straightened up, "So it is Konrad," he said softly. "Ah, well, perhaps it is for the best."

"What's that?" said Johnny in surprise.

We waited for him to go on, but after looking down at the

still body for a moment or two he turned away and went over to the police car.

"Mein General," he said, opening the rear door. "If you would be so good as to step outside . . . not the Fraulein, please. Such sights are not for young ladies."

In the dying flames from the wrecked Mercedes the General's face looked haggard and drawn. But his bearing was no less erect as he limped the few yards to join us.

"Some friends of yours, I believe, mein General," said Sergeant Müller. "And—an old enemy."

The General greeted us with real warmth but it was impossible to guess at his thoughts as he looked down at the twisted, mud-spattered body. He nodded slowly and turned to Sergeant Müller. "Your handcuffs will not be needed, Sergeant," he said.

I looked over at the police car. Grizelda had put down the side window and was looking out at the scene of devastation. I walked over. "Hallo," I said.

"What is it?" she said anxiously. "What has happened?"

"Konrad," I said briefly. "He's dead."

"Konrad? But how? And what are you doing here?"

"It's a long story, Grizelda. We thought it was over, but there was one more chapter. I gather your uncle told them everything."

"Not quite everything. I persuaded him not to speak of the letter. I thought at least we could burn that. . . ."

I nodded at the smouldering wreckage. "Konrad saved you the trouble."

"You mean—it was in his car? And the forged money?"

"The lot. And he very nearly got away with it." I hesitated. "I suppose the police had to know about that side of it—the stuff in the cave, I mean?"

She smiled enigmatically. "It seems the good sergeant didn't take Willi very seriously. Willi, he is inclined to think, sees too much television. He is not, perhaps, a very perceptive man."

"Then what were they after Konrad for?"

"Murder—and blackmail."

"But I thought you said . . ."

"They asked for no details. Their Chief is a most under-standing man. But it appears Konrad has been suspected for some time of living a double life—spending too much money, this beautiful car. They searched his apartment and found evidence that he was a professional blackmailer. Even Holtz was in his power, and this, they believe, would give Konrad a motive for killing him. They suggest Holtz was threatening to expose him and . . ."

"What a hope," I said. "Still, it's just as well. They'd have had a job to find the proof."

"They say by comparing the bullet with Konrad's gun . . ."

"They'll have a job," I said, "to find even that. Look, I'll go over and make sure Uncle Arnold isn't letting any cats out of the bag."

But the others were already coming towards us. From the wink Roger gave me I knew all was well.

"They're coming back with us," he said.

Sergeant Müller addressed himself to Grizelda. "You will appreciate, Fraulein, that I shall be occupied here for some time. In the circumstances Herr Vermont has kindly offered to convey you and the Herr General to 'der Grun Specht.' If the Fraulein is agreeable. . . ."

She got out with alacrity. "But of course, Sergeant." And then to Johnny, "If we will not be too many?"

"Too many? She's taken ten before now."

As we drove away, leaving Sergeant Müller poking dis-consolately among the smoking ruins, Roger said, "Er—could we go back the way we came? There's the Daimler, you know."

"No," said Uncle Arnold with finality. "No more to-night. I want my dinner and I'm not going to be side-tracked any more. I suggest we forget all about Konrad and Holtz and their beastly machinations and try to enjoy what's left of the evening."

"Good idea," said Johnny.

"Except," said Uncle Arnold reflectively, "that I would rather like to know which of them took a pot shot at me."

I said, "Holtz was the best shot. On the other hand Konrad was at the end of the line. He could have slipped into the trees with the least risk of being spotted. Tell you what, why don't we ask Willi."

"That's right," said Roger with relish. "Let *me* ask him."

They'd put me between Grizelda and her uncle on the back seat. "Grizelda," I said, "there's one question I'd like to ask you. It's been puzzling me all along. What was it about us that gave you such a fright when you saw us through the lounge window that first evening?"

She covered her face with her hands and at first I thought she was crying. Then she looked up and I saw that she was blushing furiously.

"But Jimmy, it was nothing about you . . ."

"No? Then what . . . ?"

She looked around in confusion. Both Uncle Arnold and Roger had turned and were waiting expectantly.

"Well, you see . . ." She hid her face again and finished in a tiny voice, "I'd been washing my hair and—and it was still in pins!"